Cate looked at him a long moment, her lovely green eyes wide and bright.

She swallowed and took another breath. "She's yours, Davian. Adella is your daughter."

He sat there, the words not really registering at first as his mind raced. Funny, it sounded like she'd said the little girl was his daughter too.

But…no. That couldn't be right. His gaze dropped to the little girl's sleeping face again, the dark hair that was so like his own. Like his father's and brother's too. And that jawline… Images of his brother when they'd been younger flashed into Davian's mind. Pictures of himself too.

You recognize it because you recognize yourself in her.

Those words stole all the breath from his lungs and his chest tightened.

Oh God.

Davian gaped, first at Cate, then Adella, then Cate again. "I don't… I… How? Why?"

He sounded ridiculous, he knew, but he couldn't seem to wrap his mind around the fact that he had a child. With Cate.

My daughter.

Dear Reader,

Welcome to my first "royals" book for the Harlequin Medical line! When I'm developing new story ideas, I always ask lots of "What if…" questions. So, for this story, I asked what would happen if I crossed Cinderella with the Bravo reality TV show *Below Deck*, then threw in a medical twist, just for fun? And voilà! *The GP's Royal Secret* was born.

This story takes place on board a luxury superyacht while sailing around the sunny Mediterranean. It has lots of fabulous destinations, royal intrigue, sizzling chemistry and adorable kids. I do hope you enjoy sailing the Mediterranean with Cate, Prince Davian and adorable Adella!

Until next time, happy reading!

Traci

THE GP'S
ROYAL SECRET

TRACI DOUGLASS

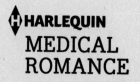

HARLEQUIN
MEDICAL
ROMANCE

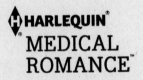

HARLEQUIN®
MEDICAL
ROMANCE™

Recycling programs
for this product may
not exist in your area.

ISBN-13: 978-1-335-73758-8

The GP's Royal Secret

Copyright © 2022 by Traci Douglass

For questions and comments about the quality of this book,
please contact us at CustomerService@Harlequin.com.

Harlequin Enterprises ULC
22 Adelaide St. West, 41st Floor
Toronto, Ontario M5H 4E3, Canada
www.Harlequin.com

Printed in U.S.A.

Traci Douglass is a *USA TODAY* bestselling romance author with Harlequin/Mills & Boon, Entangled Publishing and Tule Publishing, and has an MFA in Writing Popular Fiction from Seton Hill University. She writes sometimes funny, usually awkward, always emotional stories about strong, quirky, wounded characters overcoming past adversity to find their forever person and heartfelt, healing happily-ever-afters. Connect with her through her website: tracidouglassbooks.com.

Books by Traci Douglass

Harlequin Medical Romance

First Response in Florida

The Vet's Unexpected Hero
Her One-Night Secret

A Weekend with Her Fake Fiancé
Their Hot Hawaiian Fling
Neurosurgeon's Christmas to Remember
Costa Rican Fling with the Doc
Island Reunion with the Single Dad
Their Barcelona Baby Bombshell
A Mistletoe Kiss in Manhattan

Visit the Author Profile page at Harlequin.com.

CHAPTER ONE

PRINCE DAVIAN MICHAEL JULIAN HENRY CONSTANTINE DE LOROSO had planned all the details of this trip so carefully for his father, the King of Ruclecia, right down to the ports they would visit on their impromptu two-week-long Mediterranean cruise to the selection of crew members. Everything should have been perfect. Unfortunately, it was anything but—starting with the contrary disposition of the chef he'd hired. The chef who was currently arguing vehemently in French with the chief steward, a congenial American named Noah, as Davian intervened. He'd mastered three big *D*'s in his life—diplomacy, determination, and becoming a world-renowned doctor. Davian refused to add defeated to the list because of one irate chef.

"Listen to me," Davian said to François, the chef in question, summoning his most placating tone. The same one that he used to soothe the overblown egos of some surgeons when he taught them cutting-edge techniques to improve their skills. "Please put down the meat cleaver. Let's remain calm."

"Non," François said, pointing to Noah with the cleaver. "Not until he leaves my galley."

The galley in question was on board the *Querencia*, the mega-yacht Davian had hired for this trip. She had recently been refitted with updated technology and security features, as well as amenities, making her the obvious choice for a quick escape from a recently developing threat in their tiny island nation. Normally on yachts, even the mega ones, the kitchen facilities could be smaller and cramped. But not so with the *Querencia*. At one hundred and eighty feet, the *Querencia* was bigger and better than anything else on the sea and that went for her galley too. Sparkling tile floors, sparkling top-tier stainless-steel appliances, sparkling utensils and equipment. No expense had been spared. Nothing but the best for the royal family of Ruclecia.

At least those in line for the throne. As the spare to the heir, Davian had been regulated to second-tier status, like a built-in advisor and assistant to his family rather than a titled prince, obligated to do his duty but not overshadow those above him in the line of succession. Even so, he'd managed to carve out a life he loved for himself. He'd never wanted the power, and the headaches that came with it. He was more than content to follow his own ambitions and dreams, to help those who needed his skills as a doctor and surgeon and make the world a better place. And today, that started with keeping the peace of his well-chosen crew.

"Chef François, put down the cleaver and please explain what our chief steward said to upset you so," Davian tried again. "Was it about your menu?"

"He said my *fines ravioles potagères au consommé ambré* looked like *vomi anémique*!"

A long stream of invectives hurled in rapid-fire French followed. Davian closed his eyes and took a deep breath. Even if Davian hadn't spoken six languages, the fact that each curse was punctuated by a slam of the cleaver into the wooden carving board made it abundantly clear his highly regarded, three-starred Michelin chef was deeply offended by what was probably an offhand comment by the chief stew.

Davian had gone to medical school in America and done most of his residency there, so he understood their humor. François, on the other hand, obviously did not. Heat from the galley prickled Davian's face and neck. It had to be close to triple digits in there, with all the cooking and shouting happening. And even all the portholes being open didn't help. Most likely because they'd set off from Gibraltar earlier that morning and August in the Mediterranean had been the hottest month of the year so far.

"That's not what I said," Noah said from behind Davian. "I said perhaps they needed a bit more color before we served them to the King and Queen."

"Bâtard! Tu mens!"

"Stop!" Davian said, giving each man a stern stare. Both men had been hired because of their impeccable résumés and skills. He didn't want to fire either. Just keep them from killing each other for the duration of this cruise. Davian looked down at the plates of food ready to be delivered upon his parents' arrival and sighed. They did look a bit...bland, but then bland was what his father's health required at present. After a major heart attack and quadruple bypass surgery the previous year, King Phillipe was on a strict diet for the foreseeable future to keep his risk factors for another cardiac event low. Another reason they were on this impromptu cruise. Whispers of assassination threats tended to raise one's blood pressure considerably. Especially when the Ruclecian royal family had already lost one member to a bullet. Davian sometimes still dreamed about the day his beloved grandfather had been shot...

Another whack of the cleaver into the cutting

board jarred Davian out of his memories and back to the present situation.

"Right. Well, I think these dishes look *très bien*," he told François. "And since I am your employer, my opinion is the only one that matters."

That seemed to appease the chef, since François slowly lowered the cleaver back down to the counter, where Davian quickly claimed it. Used to handling scalpels, he found the cleaver's weight was a bit unsettling. Still, there was no way he was letting François get his hands on the thing again. Not right now, anyway.

"*Merci*, Chef," Davian said to François then turned to Noah, who still stood behind him, his expression stoic with an undercurrent of antipathy. The relationship between a chef and a chief stew was always fraught with a bit of that, Davian had learned from his years on board his father's yachts.

Almost like siblings, he thought.

Heaven knew Davian and his older brother, Arthur, had their share of issues with each other.

And while Davian had been sent to the same schools and traveled to the same places over the years as his older brother, it was always made clear that they were different. Arthur would one day become King. Davian would only ascend if something awful happened to his father and his brother, and any male children his brother might have. The royal guard and Ruclecian security forces worked day and night to make sure that never happened. Not that Davian wasn't important in the system though. He had other uses. Like playing travel agent, or diplomat, or even fiancé, when needed, only to be quickly shoved aside when the need no longer existed.

As an accomplished man with goals and dreams of his own, he was sick of it.

He'd disrupted his own life more times than he could count for his family and enough was enough. After this cruise was over and the assassination threat had passed, Davian planned to sit down with his parents and tell them he was done. No more neglecting his life and his medical career for the sake of his royal duties. He'd been through a lifetime of putting his family needs and obligations ahead of his own and now he was done. He just had to get through this last cruise first.

"Noah, once my parents and their guests have arrived and settled in, please have your staff take these plates up to them in the main dining room," Davian said in the voice he used in his operating rooms, the precise one that brooked no argument. Then he turned back to the chef. "And François, carry on with dinner preparations. No more comments from either of you on the other's performance. Understood?"

"Yes, sir," Noah grumbled, stepping forward to grab three plates while his second stew did the same.

"Oui," mumbled François.

"Good." Davian then started out of the galley in the opposite direction, toward the stairs leading up to the private cabins, where he'd been headed when this whole debacle started. He made it up two steps when an announcement crackled over the yacht's PA system from the captain.

"All medical personnel to the bridge stat. All medical personnel to the bridge for an emergency."

With a curse, Davian changed directions and sprinted back through the galley and up a different set of stairs to the bridge, adrenaline pumping again. Seemed his work was never done on this cruise.

"Mommy, what's that?"

Dr. Cate Neves gazed over at the huge limestone promontory near the southernmost tip of the Iberian Peninsula and smiled. "That, Adella, is the Rock of Gibraltar."

The five-year-old frowned, scrunching her nose up. "It's really big."

"Yes, it is." Cate chuckled then crouched beside her daughter on the deck of the *Querencia*, the luxury mega-yacht she'd been hired to act as assistant physician on for this voyage. She then turned her daughter around to face the opposite shoreline again, resting her chin on the little girl's shoulder while keeping an arm around her waist to hold her close as the wind blew around them. "See that land there? That's Morocco." Then Cate turned with Adella in her arm to face the opposite direction. "In Africa. We're currently between two continents."

"What's a continent?" Adella asked. She was full of questions these days. Same as Cate had been at that age. "And where are we going?"

"A continent is a large landmass." Cate straightened and took her daughter's hand. They'd be on board this yacht for the next two weeks and she intended to make the most of it, showing her daughter all the amazing things you could see and experience while traveling. "And we're sailing the Mediterranean for Mommy's work, remember?"

"Who do you work for, Mommy? And why do you work on a boat?" Adella tugged free and ran over to sit on one of the outdoor sofas on the *Querencia*'s uppermost deck with her new favorite stuffed animal, a monkey named Fred. She was at that age where everything was an endless stream of "why" questions.

"Well, on this cruise I work for Dr. Will." With a sigh, Cate walked over and joined her daughter, sinking into the plush royal blue cushions and staring out at the horizon. It was around noon now and the mist was finally burning off. The Spanish locals here called it *levanta* and it was common most days, what with the water and air temperatures between the colder Atlantic and the warmer Mediterranean. The sun and wind would drive it off soon enough.

Cate had learned a lot about sailing over the past five years, first by working on board cruise ships as a doctor and now in locum tenses support positions on private vessels like the *Querencia*. This was the first time, however, she'd signed on without knowing anything about the primary clients on board. They'd made her sign all sorts of nondisclosure agreements and privacy clauses. A formality, Dr. William Bryant had said. Nothing more. And the pay for this voyage was incredible, so she couldn't say no. Not if she wanted to start her own practice once she got back to the States after this last cruise. She'd been squirreling away funds since she'd graduated from Stanford medical school five years ago to make her dream come true and now it was finally so close she could taste it. And the fact that this whole job had appeared basically out of the blue… Well, it seemed like fate.

So, with just a general reassurance from Will that this cruise was above board and did not involve any mafia or oligarchs or anything, plus with the agreement that she could bring her daughter, Adella, with her, Cate had signed on the dotted line. Still, Cate couldn't help wondering who could afford to charter a ship like this, plus pay all the crew and expenses that went along with running it.

"Mommy? Do we have to go back downstairs again? I like it up here."

"I like it up here too, sweetie." She ran her fingers through her daughter's long black hair, left loose today to hang down her back in a riot of curls and clipped on the side with two rainbow barrettes. "But Mommy needs to finish stocking her clinic and you need to have some lunch, so yes. We must go back downstairs soon."

She'd taken a quick break and come up and seen the Port of Gibraltar from the uppermost deck. It was one of her favorite things since she'd first started sailing. So pretty and peaceful. Except when the wind picked up and the water got choppy, like now.

After they'd restocked supplies and fuel here at Gibraltar and the rest of the guests arrived, they'd continue into the Mediterranean, stopping in Marseille, and Monaco, before finishing in Sicily. A short, relaxing trip. And after the past five years, struggling to survive as a single mother, Cate deserved this hopefully relaxing break. Not that she wasn't working. She was. But most of the time, the worst she dealt with on these luxury trips were the occasional stomach ailment or migraine. Every so often, there'd be something more serious though, like heatstroke or cardiac issues—like the primary guest on this cruise had, according to the brief overview she'd been given by Will earlier—but hopefully, this trip would fall more on the easier side.

After one long, last glance at the gorgeous scenery, Cate stood and smoothed a hand down the front of her white shirt and pants, standard medical uniform on board the *Querencia*, before reaching for her daughter's hand. "C'mon, sweetie. Time to go."

The little girl sighed, then slid down off her seat, staring up at Cate with the same blue eyes as her father. A man she hadn't seen in five years. By choice, since he'd lied to her about who he was and left her when she'd need him most. Cate had grown up with a father like that already and didn't want or need more of that in her life now. "Can we visit that big rock while we're here, Mommy? I'd like to climb it."

Cate smiled as they started downstairs toward the crew cafeteria. "Not this time, sweetie. But maybe we can come back someday, just you and I, and spend some time here. What do you say?"

"I'd like that." Adella grinned, making Cate's

heart pinch. That grin she remembered too. In fact, she remembered everything about the man who'd deceived her about everything. But then if it wasn't for him, Cate wouldn't have her daughter, so she couldn't regret it entirely.

Adella whispered something to her stuffed monkey then said, "Fred likes it here too. And he's hungry. Can I have fruit for lunch, Mommy?"

"We'll see what the chef put out today." The yacht not only had all the amenities for its passengers, but they also had a great setup for the crew as well with the chef-prepared buffets for each meal for them. And between the stewards and the deckhands, she always had someone to watch Adella for her when Cate couldn't. She knew most of them from working together on previous cruises and considered them friends. After getting fruit for her daughter and eggs and a cup of much-needed coffee for herself from the buffet, they settled at a table near the wall to eat quickly. Cate had just sat down when the call came over the PA system.

"All medical personnel to the bridge stat. All medical personnel to the bridge for an emergency."

Cate was on her feet and signaling for one of her crewmates, a third stew named Andy. She and Cate had quickly become close friends on the *Querencia*. Andy had joined the crew to help her recover after the loss of her wife to leukemia. They'd been together for almost twenty years. Loving and losing left scars. Cate knew that from experience. Her own father had walked out on her and her mother when Cate was just ten. "Andy's going to watch you until I get back, okay? Mommy needs to go."

Cate ran down the hall to the clinic and grabbed her medic bag then raced up the stairs to the bridge. She had no idea what she'd encounter once she got there, but she'd seen plenty of emergencies during her residency in California and her work since. So much so that she'd even considered doing that as her specialty rather than general practice at one point. But life intervened and she'd needed the steady work hours being a GP provided to be there for Adella. Now, as she raced toward who knew what, her blood pumped and her heart raced and she relished the urgency.

"Dr. Cate Neves," she announced as she burst onto the bridge and weaved through the people gathered there, without really looking at them. Her complete focus was on the female crew member on the floor, apparently unconscious. She pulled out her stethoscope to check the woman's vitals. "What happened here?"

"They were cleaning the artifacts in the case over there," Captain Stan said. "She'd put on gloves to remove one of the statues and had this reaction. She's cleaned them many times before, so we thought it was fine."

Another crew member held up the box and Cate gave a curt nod.

Classic latex allergy. They often developed after repeated exposures and in some cases could become life-threatening, as appeared to be the case here. You never knew when someone might have a bad reaction, which was why Cate never used latex gloves in her practice. But she'd never lost a patient before and wasn't about to start now.

She focused on the patient again, as she dug into her bag for the EpiPen she always kept stashed there for emergencies. A quick dose of epinephrine into an anaphylactic patient helped them recover much faster. "Someone please call 112 and have an ambulance ready to take this crew member to the hospital in Gibraltar. And does anyone else here have basic medical training to assist me?"

"I do," a man said, the voice deep and oddly familiar. "I'm a doctor as well."

He weaved through the crowd on the bridge and knelt opposite Cate. She hazarded a glance up at the new arrival and...

Oh, God! No. It couldn't be.

And yet, it was. The man who'd disappeared from her life five years ago. Adella's father.

David Laurence.

At least that was the name he'd gone by during residency.

The name of the man she'd studied with, fallen in love with.

Except it was all a lie. Everything about him had been a lie.

If she hadn't been so well trained in emergency situations, Cate might have frozen. As it was, her surprise paralysis only lasted a few seconds before she snapped out of it and continued working on her patient. The woman's breathing had become more labored, and a nasty allergic rash now spread up her arms and neck. Time for the EpiPen. Cate pinched the woman's thigh and jammed the needle in to administer the lifesaving drug, then checked the woman's pulse and respirations again. Most times the results were dramatic, stopping the anaphylaxis in its tracks.

"Is the ambulance on the way?" Cate asked one of the crew standing by as she noticed the patient's breathing had become deeper and more regular already. The rash was going down too. Good signs.

Her gaze flicked up to the man across from her who was taking the patient's pulse and Cate's own heart stumbled once more. What in the hell was Adella's father, the man who'd walked out of Cate's life five years ago, doing on board the *Querencia*?

"Ambulance is here, doc," the crew member said, jarring Cate back to the present. "The medics are bringing in a gurney."

"Thank you." Cate glanced up at her ex again to find him scowling in concentration, an expression she recognized from their years of working together. He looked nearly the same as the last time she'd seen him—still tanned, toned and gorgeous. Short dark hair and cerulean blue eyes. Her chest squeezed and she looked away fast as the patient groaned, the woman's eyelids fluttering as she came around.

"Alice?" Cate patted the crew member's cheek lightly. "It's Dr. Neves. Do you remember what happened?"

The patient tried to sit up, but Cate placed a hand on the woman's chest to keep her from moving.

"N-no," Alice said, her white ship's uniform rumpled from the collapse. "Wh-where am I? Why is everyone staring at me?"

"You had an allergic reaction to the latex gloves you were wearing. Has that ever happened to you before, Alice?" Cate pulled an IV kit out of her medical bag and began swabbing the woman's arm while she waited for an answer.

"N-no. I don't have any allergies, that I'm aware of."

"Well, now you do." Cate tossed the alcohol pad she'd used into the trash then opened the IV kit. Best to put it in now so the medics could give Alice fluids on the way to the hospital. "I'll be sure to fill the medics in on what happened here so your doctor at the hospital can go over it all with you. I'm going to put another needle into your arm, Alice. You'll feel a quick stick and that's it. Okay?"

Alice nodded and Cate hit the vein on her first try then taped the cannula into place. "All done."

"Wh-why can't I remember anything?" The woman blinked up at Cate, tears forming in her eyes. "Wh-what's happening to me?"

"Disorientation is normal after an episode like yours. Don't worry, Alice. Rest now. You just had a bad reaction to the latex gloves you were wearing, but I've given you a shot of epinephrine and you should make a full recovery. We've got an ambulance here now to take you to the hospital for an all clear, just to be on the safe side."

Behind Cate, the medics arrived and brought the gurney in. She moved out of the way, giving the medics the rundown of the incident and the patient's current vitals as they got Alice started on IV fluids then prepared to take her out to the ambulance. David stayed by Cate's side, his arm occasionally brushing hers in the crowded bridge area, making a rush of unwanted awareness shimmer through her nervous system. It had always been like that between them.

Instant connection. Prolonged hurt.

Alice groaned again. "Where are they taking me?"

"To the local medical center in Gibraltar, ma'am," one of the medics said. "We'll take good care of you, I promise."

"Pulse is back in normal range and so is her b/p," the other paramedic said. "Good response to the EpiPen. Dr. Neves." The man's gaze flicked to David and widened slightly before he bowed. "And you, Your Highness."

Cate's hackles rose and she forced her tense shoulders to relax. Yes, her ex, David Laurence, had turned out to be none other than Prince Davian de Loroso of the tiny, wealthy European island nation of Ruclecia. Just one of the things he'd lied to her about when they'd been together in college, making Cate believe he was only a young, ambitious medical student like herself, working his way through school to follow his dreams. None of it was true, of course, but she'd been so naive and in love, she'd bought it hook, line and sinker, until it was too late. Even now, anger buzzed inside her, mainly at herself. Seeing what her own mother had gone through, raising Cate on her own and dealing with the heartbreak of being left behind, Cate had sworn to never be taken in like that again. It was the main reason she'd stayed on her own so long. If you didn't put yourself out there, you didn't get hurt.

"Stay calm, Alice. You're doing great. Once you get those IV fluids in your system, you'll feel a lot better and be back on board before you know it." Cate patted the woman's hand in sympathy, noting the rash on Alice's arms was nearly gone now too.

"I'll go with her to the hospital," another crew member said, stepping forward. "To make sure she makes it back before we leave port."

She waited until the patient was gone before she stooped to repack her medical bag. Davian crouched beside her to help.

"We should talk, Cate," he said, his blue gaze locked on Cate's green eyes. A myriad of emotions flitted there—shock, confusion, hurt, hesitation—though he kept his stoic facade in place the same as Cate. But it was still unsettling to find the same blue eyes her daughter Adella had inherited staring back at her now after all these years. "I… I never expected to see you today."

"That makes two of us," Cate hissed, keeping her voice low to avoid the other crew on the bridge hearing. She shoved the last items into her bag and zipped it up before straightening. "I need to get back to my clinic now."

Cate turned and left without waiting for a response from Davian. As far as she was concerned, the fact he'd vanished into thin air five years ago without even a goodbye said more than enough already.

CHAPTER TWO

AFTER THE EMERGENCY on the bridge, Davian stood at the railing of the ship, overlooking the Port of Gibraltar, enjoying a few quiet moments alone and replaying the moment he'd seen the last person he'd ever thought he'd see again—Cate Neves. It was still hard to fathom that she was on board the ship. Of all the medical clinics in all the world…

Then again, fate had thrown them together before, so he probably shouldn't be so surprised it was doing so again. Especially considering he'd hired one of their old professors from Stanford, Dr. Will Bryant, to be chief medical officer on board this cruise, and given him full authority to fill out his staff as he saw fit. Especially since Dr. Bryant had been one of the few people who'd known Davian's true identity back then…

Cate had looked as effortlessly gorgeous as he remembered. Long honey-blond hair, streaked with platinum, secured back in an efficient ponytail, her wide green eyes reminding Davian of the emerald hills of Ruclecia, and her body... the same body that had filled his fantasies for the past five years.

Cate was the one who got away.

No. More precisely, Cate was the one he'd let go. Because he'd had no choice.

Stop it.

Imagining what might have been did him no good now. For all his pragmatism and acumen, sometimes Davian's daydreams turned his own stomach. He had his duties, his career. The life he'd built for himself. He needed to be content with that. Cate had moved on, obviously, and they were different people now than they had been back in college.

Davian did wonder about her serving on a luxury yacht though. Back in residency, Cate had been focused on serving underprivileged communities and finding solutions to health disparities in underserved patient populations. Big difference between that and serving the rich and famous on yachts. Had she given up on her dreams? Changed her mind?

That didn't strike true. Cate had never been a person who gave up easily.

Most likely she'd seen the headlines of his engagement. What a joke that whole debacle had been. Arranged when Davian had barely been out of diapers to the daughter of an advantageous political ally, he'd had no say and even less choice in the matter. It had been revealed to the world when it suited his family's royal agenda. Just one more example of him being used as a pawn in a bigger game of power and PR his family participated in with the wider world. The worst thing was, Davian understood why they did it. It made sense. As the ruling family of Ruclecia, a country whose main economic engine was tourism, they needed to project a certain appearance of wealth and prestige to the rest of the world to keep people coming in. And perhaps even more importantly, he loved his family. They were good people. But they also had duties to uphold. And from the time he'd been old enough to understand such things, Davian had been taught that duty came before all else in life.

Until now, he'd believed it, lived by it.

But things had changed and his time with Cate in college had been a part of that. For the first time, he'd had a taste of what life might have been like if he'd not been royal, if he'd had the opportunity to live as others did—with freedom. Yet just when he'd thought perhaps he and Cate might have a life together after medical school, reality had landed hard on him once more. His father had fallen ill because of heart issues and Davian had been forced to flee back to Ruclecia like a thief in the night. He'd always intended to return to Cate as soon as possible, but again, his duty interceded. To throw the press off the story of his father's illness, and against Davian's will, the palace PR team had leaked news of his engagement to the press, and Davian had been forced to go through the motions of a sham engagement to Namina, his childhood arranged bride. She'd not wanted to marry him any more than he had her, but by the time his father had recovered and the engagement had been called off, it was too late. The damage had been done. He'd felt betrayed and furious. Heartbroken when he'd returned to Stanford only to find that Cate was gone. She'd graduated and moved on without him. He'd spent about a month in California, sorting through all his emotions and deciding what to do from there. He'd tried to call her, tried to make contact, but had never heard anything back from Cate. In the end, he'd finished his last few courses and graduated himself, then returned to Ruclecia alone to start over and begin his career there. For the past five years, he'd lived quietly, doing what was best for the people of his country and practicing medicine, always dreaming about the day he could walk away from the royal life when his brother became King and Davian could then immerse himself full-time in his medical career and his hospital.

He sighed and leaned his forearms on the railing, inhaling deep the sea breeze blowing in his face.

His mind still couldn't quite believe Cate was here, now, after all these years. Seeing her had been...

They'd lost so much time. There was so much water under the bridge.

Not that he could blame her for moving on from him, not after the way he'd left. Not after how he'd deceived her about his true identity. Again, that had been his father's doing, not Davian's. He'd insisted Davian attended Stanford under a false name for security reasons and Davian had agreed because he would have done anything to pursue his dreams. But still, it was no excuse for how he'd handled things with Cate. At the time, he'd thought it was for the best, but now...

Dammit.

Dredging all this up again was worthless. It was all done. Over. He needed to let it go and stay focused on the work in front of him. This cruise, his family, the upcoming talk with his parents.

Except once again, more images of Cate on the bridge filled his stubborn mind.

He pictured her as she'd knelt across from him as they locked eyes again for the first time, all the emotions flickering through her lovely eyes—surprise, hurt, anger, anxiety. How those walls of hers had slammed down again as she'd walked away from him this time. Part of him had wanted to run after her, to beg her to allow him to explain why he'd left all those years ago, but what was the point? At best, they'd have fourteen days to get reacquainted, then go their separate ways again.

No. It was better to leave things as they were. Simpler.

Since when have you ever been simple?

With a sigh, Davian straightened and fiddled with his aqua silk tie then buttoned his suit jacket. It was way too hot here to be so formal, but his parents would expect him in a suit and right now it was easier to appease than to argue about it. He glanced over at the dock as their injured crew member returned to the yacht by taxi, then saw the deckhands begin working the large mechanical metal spools to bring up the anchor so they could finally set sail. How had Cate ended up working on a yacht? Did she enjoy it? Remembering her carefree nature back in college, he suspected she would.

Making his way back toward his stateroom, he thought about working with her to help the patient on the bridge. The same awareness shimmering through his bloodstream despite the circumstances, how it had always been like that between them from the first time they'd met.

CHAPTER THREE

CATE WAS JUST finishing up restocking the supply cabinet in the yacht's small medical clinic. It was one of the guest cabins they'd quickly renovated for this charter. In her experience, most super-yachts didn't have medical personnel aboard unless the primary guests brought their own, but this trip was different. In more ways than one.

Adella was with chef François in the galley, helping him clean vegetables for dinner tonight. All the crew loved having Cate's daughter on board and everyone took turns spending days with her whenever Cate had other duties to attend to. Talk about a village to raise a child. It was one of the things Cate would miss when she left after this charter. The sense of family and close friends aboard. Even when she'd worked on the larger cruise ships when she'd first started out, that camaraderie had been there, though it was more close-knit with a smaller yacht crew. Back home in Boston, it was usually just her and Adella at the apartment, or sometimes Cate's mother too, when she came over to babysit or spend the weekend with them. Her mom and Adella were close and Cate loved seeing her mother tell Adella some of the same family stories she'd told Cate growing up or teaching her how to make some of the recipes that had been passed down for generations.

She'd just completed her daily check of the medicine cabinet and logged her results with Carrie, the clinic's receptionist, when the crew member from earlier, the one with the allergic reaction arrived.

"Hey, doc," Alice said from the doorway of the clinic. She was still a bit pale and her expression sheepish, but otherwise a thousand times better than when she'd left that morning. "Got the all clear to return."

Cate took the discharge papers the woman handed her and glanced over them. "Good. Everything looks fine on here, though I'd advise you take it easy the rest of the day, just to be sure. And stay away from anything latex from here on out, yeah?"

"Will do, doc," Alice said, tucking the papers Cate handed her back into the pocket of her uniform pants. "So weird that it hit me out of nowhere. Never had that happen before."

"Not uncommon for them to build up over

time until one day it becomes life-threatening. I've seen it happen with nuts and beestings before too."

"Wow." Before Alice could say anything more, the walkie-talkie on her belt crackled to life and Captain Stan's voice issued forth.

"Captain to Alice. Captain to Alice. Report to the bridge ASAP."

Alice exhaled and shrugged. "Guess it's back to duty for me."

"Guess so," Cate said, smiling. "Don't work too hard."

"I won't, doc." Alice waved before walking away. "See you later."

"Always."

Cate returned to cleaning the clinic and getting it ready for the new set of guests who'd be boarding soon. She didn't know anything about their identities other than their basic medical histories. Both were in their sixties. The woman was healthy with only the normal hypertension and arthritis issues typically seen in patients that age. The man, however, had serious cardiac problems post–quadruple bypass surgery the previous year. He was on a variety of medications and was regularly checked by a top-notch cardiologist. Cate was anxious to meet her patients and get to know the people she'd be caring for this charter. Or at least she had been until David had shown up.

Not David. Davian.

Why did he have to appear after all these years? After she and Adella had made a life for themselves, independent of him and everything that had happened in the past. Seeing him there on the bridge had been like a sucker punch, stealing her breath and freezing her mind. Luckily, she'd snapped out of it quickly and been able to save the patient.

With Davian's help…

She sighed and hung her head. He'd always been an excellent physician, regardless of what happened between them, and she probably ought to apologize to him for walking away like she had. Five years had passed, so she should be over it by now, right?

Except how exactly did you get over something like that?

In her case, you didn't.

But now she was worried because if Davian was here, aboard the *Querencia*, did that mean he was sailing with them too? Over the years, Cate had worried about the implications of royalty after she'd discovered Davian's true identity. What she knew about how all that worked could fill a thimble, but some internet research did show that as the child of a second son, and the fact that Davian's older brother was married and had two children of his own, it was highly unlikely that Adella would ever be heir of Ruclecia. Still, Davian had been swept back to his country in the middle of the night and engaged within a week—not to mention all the deception and secrecy surrounding his identity and his security—and Cate wanted no part of that for her daughter. So, she'd kept all that from Adella, not really telling her anything about her father. Up until now, it hadn't been a problem, since Cate had doubted she'd ever see Davian again. Except as Adella got older, she'd started asking more questions about who her father was and where he was. And now Davian had appeared in Cate's life again out of the blue and...

What a mess.

Cate had become a shipboard doctor to get away from her past and start fresh, but now she was trapped out at sea with her past for the next two weeks. She sighed and stared up at the ceiling as more memories flooded back.

She'd been so sick those first few weeks of her pregnancy that searching for David had taken everything she'd had. When she'd seen his face splashed all over the news with the story of his upcoming nuptials, her heart had shattered. How could he do that to her? They'd been friends and work colleagues before they'd ever been lovers.

They'd talked together, studied together. Cate had felt closer to Davian than anyone else in her life besides her mother. He'd told her he felt the same. So how in the world could he have made love to her, taken their relationship to the next level, knowing he was engaged to another woman? Her heart still ached over that, even five years on. She'd thought David was different, not like her father. Honorable and true. But apparently that wasn't the case at all. Cate had allowed desire and passion to cloud her logic. She'd vowed never to make that mistake again.

By the end of her third trimester, Cate had felt more like herself and accepted the fact David was gone for good. He'd lied about his royal status and the fact she'd been turned away like so much trash told her exactly what she needed to know—that even if he'd told her the truth about who he was, she wasn't good enough to be part of his world. Fine. She'd been independent her whole life and she'd continue to make it on her own. Leaving California behind and making the decision to take to the sea once she'd had Adella had been the best choice Cate had ever made. The money was good, and she got to travel all over the world and show her daughter around all the exotic places they visited. She wouldn't have traded it for anything. That kind of education was priceless.

She didn't need David anymore. She had worked hard the past five years to build the life she'd planned for her and Adella and after this charter she would finally reach her goal of opening her own family practice outside Boston. She'd saved enough money to put a down payment on property and had already researched all the equipment and staff she'd need. Luxury cruises were nice, but her dream had always been to help those most in need and now she could do that full-time. No way would she let Davian derail her again. Even if he still made her pulse trip the same way it always had around him.

"Hey," a voice said from the doorway and Cate looked back to see Noah there with Adella. "Someone's looking for their mom."

"Mommy!" Adella said, running over to jump into Cate's arms and hug her tight around the neck as Cate picked her up and buried her face in her daughter's hair, inhaling the good smell of baby shampoo and sea. "I got to hold a parsnip!"

"Really?" Cate leaned back and grinned at the little girl, then glanced over to Noah. "Thanks for bringing her back."

"No problem. Cap says we need to be on deck in our whites to greet the new guests in five minutes."

"Thanks." Cate carried Adella out into the hall and down a set of spiral stairs to the crew deck and put her in their cabin. Most crew members shared cabins, with bunk beds in each and a small bathroom. But because Cate was traveling with her daughter, they put them in their own cabin. She got Adella settled on the bottom bunk and turned the small TV on for her. "You okay here until Mommy gets done?"

"Yep," Adella said, already occupied with changing one of her doll's outfits. "All good."

"Great." Cate checked her appearance in the mirror. Thankfully, she'd already dressed in her whites this morning in preparation for the guests' arrival. She walked out of the head and kissed the top of her daughter's head before exiting the cabin and hurrying up to the main deck just in time to see a small convoy of three black SUVs with black tinted windows arrive at the dock. Two men got out of the first truck dressed in black suits and sunglasses, clearly bodyguards. They spoke into devices in their ears as they checked the area then were joined by four more men in black from the third SUV. All six men formed a perimeter around the middle SUV as the driver got out and opened the doors to reveal an older couple.

The crew of the *Querencia* had been trained not to gawk at their sometimes famous guests but it was difficult when those guests turned out to be none other than the King and Queen of Ruclecia.

Oh, boy.

Cate's stomach lurched and her mind raced. Davian's parents were here. Which explained why he was on board. But she would have thought that they would have owned a private yacht of their own. That would seem the most secure choice. She obviously wasn't the only one thinking this as a low murmur passed through the crew. Her second thoughts were of Adella. Having the King and Queen aboard meant more chance of someone recognizing her striking resemblance to Davian. Cate felt a bit light-headed at the ramifications. She had some money saved, but not nearly enough to wage a custody fight with royalty.

An urge to grab her daughter and run away was stopped by the approach of the royal couple on the red carpet spread on the dock leading to the ship. Davian stepped out on the main deck and joined his parents on the passerelle to escort them aboard. Cate's heart sank to her toes.

This was not going to go well.

As the party made their way down the receiving line of crew members, Cate hazarded a glance at Davian and found him staring stoically ahead at the wall of the yacht in front of him. He looked about as miserable as Cate felt.

"And this is the ship's physician, Dr. Cate Neves," Davian said as he and his parents reached her. Having watched the other crew members before her, Cate bent into an awkward curtsy.

"Your Majesties," she said.

When she straightened, Cate locked gazes with Davian and her mouth dried. Blood pounding in her ears and, her knees wobbly, she kept her smile in place through sheer force of will until the King and Queen moved on to Noah beside her.

The rest of the day passed in a bit of a blur, and Cate thought perhaps she could get through this by just keeping her head down and concentrating on her work and Adella. But when she fell asleep that night, her dreams were tangled. She was lost and alone. She could see Davian in the distance, but he wasn't looking at her. She couldn't get his attention, couldn't call out for help.

She woke early, tears on her cheeks. She got up and got dressed then got Adella ready. Despite sleeping, she felt exhausted. Sunshine spilled in through the porthole in their cabin and she could hear the deck crew outside as they secured the yacht to the dock in Marseille. They'd traveled through the night to arrive at their first port of call. The *Querencia* creaked and strained against her moorings.

She wondered about Davian's homeland of Ruclecia. From the research she'd done on the place when trying to contact Davian about Adella years ago, it was a gorgeous island nation, filled with green farmland and rugged cliffs dropping off into the Baltic Sea below. Cate had spent hours online clicking through pictures of their coastlines and beautiful medieval architecture. Ruclecians spoke German, English and a smattering of Italian and French. And apparently, their royal family was far more famous than Cate had realized.

The nation had been founded centuries ago as a stronghold for spices and teas from China and their monarchy had become incredibly wealthy because of it. Now the majority of the island nation's GDP came from tourism, along with fishing, farming and clean energy. There were also casinos and horse racing, like they had in Monaco, and Ruclecia was now another tax haven for the world's wealthy.

Which again begged the question: Why were they here?

She sighed as she led Adella down to the galley for breakfast. The simplest thing to do would be to ask Davian, but that would mean talking to him again and Cate wanted to avoid that as much as possible. She had no interest in talking to him—at least for now. Bad enough she had to deal with his parents this cruise, but that was her job. She was paid to do that. Deal with the man who'd broken her heart? Not so much. Yes, eventually, she'd have to confront him and tell him the truth about Adella, but she wanted to wait. Take a little more time to get her own head on straight about it all before she said anything to him.

"Noah!" Adella called and pulled free of Cate's hand as they entered the crew mess and ran over to the chief stew. "I put a new outfit on Jenny! Do you like it?"

Adella held her doll up so the man could see and Noah gushed over the mismatched pink-and-orange ensemble appropriately before catching Cate's eye and winking.

"Stunning!" he said, placing a hand over his heart. "She'll be going to the Met Gala before you know it."

"Met Gala?" Adella scrunched her nose. "What's that?"

As Noah explained the elaborate fundraising party for the New York art museum, Cate went over to get food for her and her daughter, her mind still stuck in the past. She could still remember the day she'd decided to try being a cruise ship physician. Her mother had suggested it after seeing how unhappy Cate was stuck in Boston after Adella was born. Trying to work and be a parent was tough enough and then doing it all with a broken heart had been eating her alive inside. So, Cate's mom had shown her an ad for yacht crew training coming up in Connecticut. At first, she'd been skeptical, but then she'd called about it on a whim and soon she was enrolled. After graduation, she met with two different big cruise lines and was hired the same day. Good pay, no living expenses, free travel, and she'd been able to either take Adella with her or leave her back with her mother. Back then there'd been no downside.

Now though, after four years, Cate was ready to put down roots again. And follow her dreams.

She loaded a tray up with coffee and toast for herself and cereal and milk for Adella then went back to the table. The fact was Davian and his family were there, and she couldn't do anything about that. But she could do something about how she handled it. She'd remain professional but distant and hopefully get through this with as little turbulence as possible. And with all the usual activities and tours the interior crew normally planned for guests on these charters, it was likely she and Davian would see very little of each other. She could keep Adella out of the guest areas and with her down in the clinic. And with Davian's father's medical conditions well controlled already, it seemed unlikely he'd require her services much during the trip.

Once they docked back in Gibraltar, she'd be home free. It was good this was her last charter. Now all she had to do was figure out when, during the next two weeks, she'd sit down with Davian and tell him the truth about his daughter.

Davian woke that morning with purpose. First on his list of priorities, talk to Cate and explain his abrupt disappearance five years ago. He'd asked the captain about the clinic hours last night after dinner and wanted to get there early before Cate got busy and found another reason to avoid him.

He reached the lower deck and headed toward the door at the end of the hall. The yacht must've been recently refitted because everything looked and smelled brand-new—plush carpets, gleaming hardwood paneling, recessed lighting, gold fixtures. He'd just about reached the door to the clinic when it opened suddenly. Cate appeared. Her eyes widened slightly, and her expression fell. Before she could disappear back inside the clinic, Davian rushed forward to stop her. "Cate. Please wait. I just want to talk."

"I'm busy," she mumbled, trying to shut him out, but he wedged his foot in the door, preventing her from closing it on him. He wasn't usually aggressive like this where women were concerned, but it felt like fate that they'd been thrown together like this after all this time, and he didn't want to waste his chance. "You'll have to make an appointment."

"Why? So you can cancel it?" he asked.

He heard her curse under her breath from the other side of the door, then she whispered something to someone else. That gave Davian pause. Did she really have a patient in there? Oh, God. Now he felt awful. He'd not meant to disrupt her life—he just wanted to talk to her, put their past to rest.

Then Cate came out and closed the clinic door behind her, herding him back down the hall to the stairs. They climbed back up and Davian asked, "Where are we going?"

"Sundeck," she said, her tone as clipped as her steps. Yep, she was pissed. Davian couldn't blame her. Even more reason to have this conversation now and clear the air since they'd be stuck on this charter together for the next two weeks. No sense making it any more awkward than it had to be. Besides, he missed her. He always had. Cate led him across the bright, deserted space and over to the railings at the front of the deck. Her hair was secured back in a bun at the base of her neck this morning, but a few strands had come loose to blow in the breeze. She slipped on a pair of mirrored aviator sunglasses, masking her eyes from him, and stared out to sea. "Why are you here? You're a prince. You probably own twenty yachts of your own. So why did you rent one, Your Highness?"

The title had never set well with him and made him grit his teeth. "We don't need to be formal, Cate."

"Oh, I think we do," she said, glancing his way, reflecting his determined expression back to him. "Because if I call you what I want to, you wouldn't like that any better. Trust me."

He deserved that. Davian exhaled slowly. This was not going how he'd wanted at all. He tried again. "I want you to know how sorry I am about how things ended between us back in residency. I'd like to explain why I left the way I did after—"

"I don't care." Her tone slammed down like a wall between them. "It doesn't matter now anyway."

"It matters to me."

Cate gave a derisive snort. "I'm glad something does."

He managed to suppress a wince, barely, as her barb hit its mark. He'd lived with the guilt over leaving her that night without any word or warning, not even a goodbye, for the past five years. But he'd had no choice. Back then he'd been at the mercy of his parents and after the close call with his brother's life they'd feared the worst. Now Davian was thirty-six and his own man. He was through ripping his life apart for the benefit of others.

"I need to get back to my clinic," Cate said then, turning to walk away. "Enjoy the rest of your trip, Prince Davian."

"Cate, please," he said, rushing after her to block her path down the stairs. "Let's get all this out in the open. I don't want to let it fester anymore." When she crossed her arms and didn't budge, he added, "Please. It won't take long. I just would like a chance to apologize and explain myself, then I'll let you be."

A beat passed. Two. Three. So long that Davian feared they might still be standing there two weeks later. Even though he couldn't see her eyes, he felt that penetrating green gaze burning a hole through him anyway.

Finally, she huffed out a breath and threw her hands up. "Fine. Let's get this over with. I'm busy."

She turned on her heel and headed back to the railing while Davian bit back a smile. Regardless of the tension between them, damn it was good to see Cate again. He'd missed her. Hadn't realized how much until now. They'd been more than lovers. They'd been best friends. She'd understood him as no one else had and he'd lost a part of himself when he'd lost her. Now he'd found that piece again and he'd do whatever he could to make amends. He followed her to the railing and leaned his forearms on it, facing the Mediterranean as she was. Seemed easier that way, dulling the sharp ache of the past a bit.

Davian took a deep breath for courage and opened his mouth to start, but never got the chance.

"Mommy! Noah took me down on the dock and I made a new friend on the dock. This is Paulo. Can we play up here with you?"

CHAPTER FOUR

CATE DID HER best to hide her alarm at Adella appearing at possibly the worst possible time, but feared she'd not done a good job of it, if the curious look on Davian's face was any indication. "Uh, yes. That's fine, honey." She hurried over to where the children were playing on the deck and crouched down, all too aware of Davian's gaze tracking her every movement. "And hello, Paulo. You must be Juan's son."

"*Sí,*" the little boy said, grinning up at her and showing his missing two front teeth. Juan was one of the mechanics who worked in the engine room. He was from Spain and had custody of Paulo for the summer. Since accommodations had been made for Cate to bring Adella on, the captain did the same for Juan and his son. They shared a cabin just down the hall from Cate's.

She smiled and straightened, walking back over to where Davian still stood at the railing, watching the kids closely. His azure gaze quickly returned to her though, full of questions.

Tell him.

But she wasn't ready. Not yet. Not after everything she'd been through the past five years raising a child on her own. So, instead, she said, "Things change, as you know."

A flicker of hurt crossed his handsome face. Cate regretted her words instantly, but it was too late. They were already out there. She sighed and looked away, gentling her tone. "Your life has changed too. Wife, family of your own."

"I'm not married."

Oh.

Honestly, after the whole nightmare early in her pregnancy of trying to contact him then finding out about his engagement through the tabloids, Cate had steered very clear of any news related to the royals. Much less painful that way. She'd assumed he'd gotten married, had a family of his own now, was happy with his life. But based on his solemn expression and his blunt statement, that wasn't the case.

"I'm sorry," she said, meaning it. The kids' giggles as they chased each other around the circular hot tub in the middle of the deck was at odds with their serious conversation. "How long have you been divorced?"

"I'm not divorced either."

Now Cate felt terrible. "I'm so sorry for your loss. I had no idea."

Davian cursed under his breath then looked over at her. "I was never married, Cate. Namina and I called off the engagement shortly after it was announced. I figured you knew, since it was all over the press, but..." His voice trailed off and he looked away, raking a hand through his already messy hair. Her heart pinched at the sight of it, same as it always used to back in college. Cate quickly pushed it aside though. Now wasn't the time to get nostalgic over what might have been. He took a deep breath and focused on her again. "It's obvious to me now that you didn't know." Davian shook his head. "I should have called you right away, Cate. I know that now. But back then everything was so turbulent and then too much time had passed, and I didn't think I had the right. Plus, the last thing I wanted to do was bring you into all my family drama. I thought time would make it better. But time only caused more chaos between us, it seems."

He was right. Time had not been their friend. And while she still felt woefully unprepared for this conversation, it seemed like a now-or-never-type deal. She nodded. "Fine. Let's sit down over here and you can tell me your side of things. We can—"

Before they took a step though, a scream tore

through the air and both Cate and Davian sprang into action without a second thought. Heart pounding, she made a beeline toward the children, panic squeezing her throat tight. If anything happened to Adella…

They rounded the hot tub and found poor Paulo on the wooden deck, pale and seemingly unconscious, a small puddle of blood near his head.

"What happened?" Cate asked, kneeling in front of her daughter, and pulling the shaking, crying little girl into her arms. "Are you okay?"

"We were playing tag and I was trying to get away. The deck was slick because of the water, and he slipped and hit his head. Mommy, is he okay?" Adella buried her face in Cate's neck and cried hard.

Footsteps pounded up the stairs and soon several other crew members stood around them, looking stricken as Davian assessed the boy's condition.

"Pulse is steady, and breathing is normal," Davian said. "We need an ambulance, please. And someone get his father."

One of the deck crew raced back down the stairs to get Juan from the engine room while Cate passed Adella off to Noah so she could assist Davian. She glanced at her watch then carefully helped him turn the boy onto his back.

"From the time we heard the scream, he's been out three minutes."

Davian patted the boy's cheek. "Paulo. Paulo, can you hear me? I need you to wake up."

"Santo Christo!" Juan gasped as he ran up the stairs and knelt next to his son. "What's happened to him?"

"He and Adella were playing tag and he slipped on the wet deck around the hot tub and hit his head," Cate said, fresh guilt welling up inside her. Already Davian had become a distraction again. One she didn't need.

Thankfully, the boy began to stir, his eyelids fluttering before opening. Paulo groaned and squinted up at Cate.

"Paulo, *mi hijo.*" Juan hugged Paulo's hand to his heart. Paulo tried to sit up, but Davian placed a hand on his chest, keeping him lying flat on the deck.

"My head…" Paulo started to say.

"You slipped," Davian said, checking the boy's pulse again. "Do you remember, Paulo?"

"No." Paulo frowned. Tears welled in his eyes and his breath caught.

Juan leaned in to kiss his son's cheek and whispered something in Spanish to him that seemed to calm him down as the ambulance arrived and once again the EMTs boarded the *Que-*

rencia. Twice in two days. Cate thought that had to be a record.

Davian didn't miss a beat, suggesting he'd kept up his medical training as Cate had, after leaving Stanford. He gave them the rundown quickly and efficiently. "We have a..." He glanced at Juan. "How old is your son?"

"Seven."

"We have a seven-year-old boy who slipped and fell on the deck, hitting his head against the side of the hot tub here, and lost consciousness for about three minutes. Pulse is strong bilaterally and respirations normal."

One of the EMTs moved in to help Cate continue to examine Paulo while Davian monitored the boy's vitals. That fact that it could so easily have been Adella lying there made Cate shudder.

I should've been watching them more closely. I shouldn't have let myself get distracted by Davian and all the drama between us.

"Can you tell me if anything hurts, Paulo? Besides your head?" Cate asked.

The little boy shook his head. "I want my papa."

"He's right here," she said. "And he'll be with you when we take you to the hospital too, okay?"

Paulo's bottom lip quivered but he didn't start crying again. Brave boy. He gave a little nod as

Cate began palpating his neck. "How about here? Does this hurt?"

"Ow!" Paulo scowled. "*Sí*. That hurt."

"Okay." Cate began examining the little boy's head, no easy feat considering the thick dark hair obscuring Paulo's scalp. "Looks like we have a two-centimeter laceration over the right parietal skull area. No evidence of fracture at this point but they'll probably want to do a CT to confirm."

"Can you open your mouth for me?" Davian asked the boy, and Paulo did so. "Very good. There's good maxillary stability." He continued palpating over the boy's shoulders and down his arms. "Any pain here?"

"I can't feel my arm," Paulo said, his dark brows knitting.

Davian and Cate exchanged curt nods then Cate looked back over her shoulder at Juan. "That's normal with these types of injuries. Usually a temporary pinched nerve. Should go away in a little while, but the hospital will check, just in case."

Juan made the sign of the cross and Davian coaxed a little smile from Paulo by telling him a knock-knock joke as he slipped a neck brace into place around the boy's neck. He'd always had great bedside manner with patients, especially children, Cate remembered.

"Okay." Cate and Davian moved aside to let

the EMTs in with a body board they'd brought on board to transport little Paulo. "These men are going to lift you up onto this so we can get you off the boat, okay, Paulo? You just stay still."

The boy closed his eyes again. "I'm dizzy."

"I know," Cate said, her voice low and soothing. "But we're almost done here and then we'll get you all fixed up and you'll feel lots better."

"I'm going with him," Juan said, his expression anxious as he watched the EMTs carefully lift his son onto the board then secure him for transport. "Papa's right here, *mi hijo.*"

Then, as quickly as the emergency began, it cleared, leaving only the EMT's voice as he radioed into the hospital echoing behind them as they moved Paulo off the boat and the rest of the crew returned to their stations. Soon, it was just Cate and Adella and Davian alone again on the sundeck. She picked up her daughter and walked over to one of the bench seats near the railing and sat down, holding her close.

"Is Paulo gonna die?" Adella asked between sniffles.

"What?" Cate blinked away tears of her own, smiling. "No, sweetie. He'll be fine. They just need to take him to the hospital to patch him up. That's all."

"I was scared, Mommy," Adella said, burying her face in Cate's chest.

Cate rested her chin atop her daughter's head, her heart aching with the sweetness. "I know, sweetie. I was scared too. Life is like that sometimes. But we get through it by doing the hard things and having courage to keep moving anyway. And you were so brave right now. Paulo too."

Adella didn't respond, just held on to Cate tighter.

Davian came over and sat next to them. He hadn't said a word since the EMTs had left, though Cate knew from his pensive expression that the wheels were turning in his head. She just hoped they weren't turning in the direction of Adella and how much she looked like him.

To forestall any questions, she said, "You did good work there with him. You're still practicing then?"

"Thank you," he said, his tone quiet. "And yes. I run a teaching hospital in Ruclecia now, training the next generation of internists and helping all the patients I can."

"That's great." She adjusted her daughter on her lap and leaned back. "Hopefully poor Paulo won't be away long."

"I don't think he'll have any lasting issues," Davian said, scrubbing a hand over his face, his gaze on Adella now. Cate's heart fell. "You have a child."

Vocal cords tight with tension, she responded, "Yes."

"Congratulations. I know you always wanted kids. What's her name?"

"Adella."

"Lovely name for a lovely girl." He smiled and Cate's chest pinched with bittersweet memories. That crooked little grin of his always had made her knees go weak. "How old is she?"

Cate hesitated. If she told him the truth, it would be easy enough for Davian to work out the dates. But she couldn't lie to him either. She took a deep breath then answered. "Five."

"Hmm," he said, not seeming to register it at first. Then, slowly, his smile faltered, and his dark brows knitted. "I see." He looked away at last, his features tight. "You moved on quickly after I left."

Easier to seize on her anger then, Cate held Adella tighter. "After you disappeared, you mean. What was I supposed to do? Pine for you forever?"

He exhaled slow and hung his head. "No, Cate. Of course not. I didn't mean it that way. I just…" Davian shook his head. "We missed so much, you and me. So much time, so many possibilities for the future. All because of my family and my duty."

"Why didn't you just tell me who you were?

Why did you lie to me? Lead me on like that when you were never available to begin with? I thought you cared about me, Davian. I thought you were my friend."

At first, Davian just blinked at her. The edge of hurt in her tone cut deeper than any scalpel ever could because it was true. They had been friends. More than friends. And he had cared for her. Still did, truth be told, even if he'd never act on that now. Too much time had passed. They were different people now, despite the lingering thread of connection between them.

But the time had finally come for him to tell her the truth. He took a deep breath and began.

"I did try to contact you, Cate. After my engagement ended and my father's health cleared. But as I said, things in my world were chaotic and I didn't want to bring all that drama into your life—especially after disrupting it so much already…" He sighed and stared out at the horizon. "I should have done better. And I'm sorry. About all of it. Lying was never my idea and I'm so sorry you were hurt because of it, Cate. That was never my intention." When she just stared at him, holding her daughter closer, he continued. She wasn't going to make this easy and that was her prerogative. Time to put it all out there for her, at last. "The whole charade started when

I wanted to go to medical school in the States. Ruclecia has some fine institutions, but all the cutting-edge medicine was happening in America back then. I wanted to be part of that, wanted to learn everything I could there and bring it back home to Ruclecia to help my homeland." He gave a sad little snort. "My father, of course, hated the idea. Not that I'm all that important in the scheme of the royal family at home, but I am the stand-in."

"Stand-in?" Cate scowled. "I don't understand."

"I'm the spare to the heir. Insurance, in case something happens to my brother, Crown Prince Arthur. But since both my father and my brother—and any heirs my brother might have—need to be taken out before the throne would fall to me, most of my time is spent waiting."

"Waiting?"

"Yes. Waiting for something that's never going to happen, waiting for orders about what they want me to do, where I'm needed next, what mess it's become my job to clean up. But after I got into Stanford, I was through with waiting. I wanted to do something more with my life than just wait around for catastrophe or averting the next calamity to befall my family at the hands of the tabloids. I wanted to help people, make a real difference. So, I went to my father and we struck a deal. He'd let me go to America to school if I took security with me and used a false name so no one would know my true identity. Well, other than a few school officials who needed that information for my credentialing. At that time, I jumped on it."

Cate kissed the top of her daughter's head then exhaled a long breath. "Okay. So, you took a fake name and came to the US. Still doesn't explain why you didn't tell me the truth, Davian. I thought you trusted me. I trusted you. We…" Her voice trailed off as she made a vague gesture between them. "We were as close as two people could be. We spent all that time together. Working, studying, other…things."

"I know." He inhaled deep and ran a hand through his wind-tousled dark hair. "And I would have told you, Cate. I swear. In fact, I was planning to the next morning after we…" *Made love.* The words stuck in his throat, still tender after all these years. Because if he was honest with himself, he had loved Cate, more than anyone else he'd ever met. But duty had called, and he couldn't refuse back then. Today, however, the only duty he had was to the woman beside him, to explain his past actions as best he could. "I got a call, Cate. Or rather Grigorio got a call."

"Wait." Her brows knit. "You mean Greg, your roommate?"

Davian gave a curt nod. "His real name is Grigorio. He's been my valet since we were both boys. We grew up together."

"So, he works for you?"

"Did, yes," Davian said. "He's since left royal service to start his own company. Anyway, Grigorio received a call in the middle of the night from my mother telling him that I needed to return to Ruclecia. My father had had a massive heart attack and his life hung in the balance. My brother was already being prepared to ascend the throne, if needed, and I was to rush home to deal with fallout of that situation and assist with the transition of power, as was my duty. I tried to get them to allow me to stay until at least the morning so I could explain to you what was happening, but there was no time to waste. Grigorio and I packed quickly and were whisked away by the security team to a private jet and flown home all within the span of a few hours. When I left the apartment, you were still asleep. I thought I'd get to phone you the next day and talk to you, but then when I arrived in Ruclecia it was chaos. Between my family working 24/7 to keep the news out of the press and my father's condition being touch-and-go, there was barely time eat and sleep, let alone have a much-needed conversation."

A beat passed, then two. Finally, Cate asked, "And what about your engagement?"

Davian gave a harsh chuckle. "It was a publicity stunt. Namina never wanted to marry me any more than I wanted to marry her. It was all arranged when we were both toddlers. We barely knew each other. The only reason that juicy little false tidbit was leaked to the press—without my permission—was to throw the spotlight off my father's illness. My mother thought that a royal wedding was just the thing to keep the public distracted. And if it screwed up my life and plans? Well, that was too bad but all in service to the almighty crown. We de Lorosos have a long history of throwing the press off our scent. Probably started with my grandfather's assassination."

Cate looked stunned. "I'm sorry. I had no idea."

"It happened a long time ago," he said, exhaling slowly. "I was only five when it happened. Some fringe political group planned it around a story in the press about my grandfather attending the opening of a new government building in our country's capital. They shot him on national television, in front of everyone. It was awful."

"Oh, Davian." Cate reached over and placed her hand atop his, her skin warm and soft. "How terrible."

"I just remember the whole country being sad

and everyone wearing black armbands in honor of him. But after that, new rules were put in place. The press was no longer a close ally and members of the royal family never travel together in the same contingent." Cate frowned and he smiled. "Well, almost never. This is a special case," Davian said, connecting the dots for her. "The fringe political group I mentioned in regard to my grandfather never went entirely away, just underground for decades. They recently resurfaced, making new threats against us. With my father's recent health crisis and rumors of him stepping down and allowing my brother to take over the throne, the palace security team decided it might be best to get them out of Ruclecia for a while. Normally, we would have used one of the royal yachts for such a trip, but they wanted to make doubly sure that this trip was conducted as incognito as possible, so we rented the *Querencia* instead. We hope to make it the whole trip before our ruse is discovered."

Cate sat back, her shoulders relaxing a tad. "Well, at least I have a better understanding about all the secrets and false names now."

Davian leaned into the cushions beside her, their shoulders brushing slightly and sending a fresh wave of awareness through his system before he tamped it down. "It's still no excuse for how I left things back in college, Cate, and there aren't enough apologies in the world to cover it. But yes. It was all a sham, Cate. The engagement, the wedding preparations. All of it. Namina never loved me, and I never loved her. As I said, we broke things off amicably as soon as my father recovered. It was all done to throw the press off the story of my father's health. I mean, I've grown up with it and I still feel manipulated by the palace press machine and all the duties to king and country I'm expected to put before my own wants and needs. I can't imagine what someone from the outside must think of us."

"Hmm," she said, a touch of wariness lingering in her tone. Davian couldn't blame her. Maybe after some time to absorb it all she would come to see that he too had been nothing but a pawn in his family's royal games and be able to at least understand why he'd done what he'd done, even if she couldn't forgive him. "That explains a lot, actually. About you, I mean."

Now it was his turn to frown. "How so?"

One side of her pink lips quirked up into a smile and he couldn't stop his gaze from flicking there before returning to her eyes. Memories of how those lips had felt beneath his flooded his mind before he forced them away, swallowing hard.

Stop it.

"Well, you never really sounded like any of

the other med students I knew," Cate said, shrugging. "You always had a kind of...*formal* speech pattern."

"Formal?"

"Yeah. Like someone whacked you upside the head with a dictionary or something."

Davian chuckled. "I've heard that before."

They sat there in silence for a few moments, just the warm breeze and the call of seagulls around them. He'd said his piece and thought that would lessen the tension in the air, but there still seemed to be so much lingering, so much left to discuss.

"I—" he started at the same time Cate said, "We need—"

"Sorry," Davian said. "Go ahead."

"No, no. You go."

Cate adjusted her daughter again, the girl now sound asleep. Adella. Such a pretty name for a pretty girl. Long, curly hair and dark lashes fanned atop her tiny cheeks. There seemed something familiar about her features that Davian couldn't quite place, though he supposed that was to be expected with Cate being her mother and all.

When neither of them spoke, the awkwardness grew stronger, until Cate finally asked, "So, you're cruising with your family now?"

"Yes." Davian stared out at the passing coastline. "I'm here to cater to my parents' every whim."

"And act as hero," Cate added. When Davian glanced sideways at her, she smiled, genuine this time, and warmth flooded his bloodstream, making his pulse trip. Man, he'd missed that smile. "You've intervened twice now in medical emergencies, Dr. de Loroso. Thank you for your help."

"My pleasure, Dr. Neves." He grinned back and it was like the years fell away and they were back in medical school again. During both emergencies, they'd fell right back into their old routines, working like a synchronous, harmonious team. So good. So right. His chest ached with yearning to continue that easy partnership. It was rare enough in the workplace, let alone in one's personal life. Yet he and Cate had fallen into that naturally. Like they were meant to be together.

Until you weren't.

Those last words acted like a bucket of cold water on his fond memories, jarring him back to reality.

After checking his watch, Davian got up to peer over the railing and down to the bow of the ship where the deckhands were preparing for docking at their next destination, Mallorca. "I, uh, I should get back to the salon and check on my parents. Make sure everything is all right with them." He turned back to Cate. "Thank you for talking to me and letting me explain what happened. I appreciate it."

He'd hoped for a quick escape, time to ponder his thoughts and figure out where to go from here, but it was short-lived as Cate stopped him before he reached the stairs.

"Wait, Davian." She remained on the bench seat and beckoned him back. "There's something I need to tell you too."

He walked back over and sat down again. He owed her this much, considering she'd listened to him before. And given that he'd vanished out of her life without a word, there wasn't much she could say to him to shock him at this point. Cate had always been the most honest, straightforward person he'd ever known. Whatever she had to say, he knew he could trust her.

She inhaled deep, staring down at her daughter instead of looking at him, uncharacteristically nervous. "I'm not sure how to say this, honestly."

Davian laughed congenially. "From someone who has experience saying difficult things, getting it out there quickly and decisively is the best course of action."

Cate looked at him a long moment, her lovely green eyes wide and bright, then she said, "It's about Adella." She swallowed and took another breath. "She's yours, Davian. Adella is your daughter."

He sat there, the words not really registering at first as his mind raced. Funny, it sounded like she'd said the little girl was his daughter too. But that couldn't be correct. They'd only had the one night together and they'd been careful. Cate had told him she was on the pill, and he'd used a condom as well, so…

Neither is one hundred percent effective, his medical brain supplied.

But…no. That couldn't be right. His gaze dropped to the little girl's sleeping face again, the dark hair that was so like his own. Like his father's and brother's too. And that jawline… Images of his brother when they'd been younger flashed into Davian's mind. Pictures of himself too.

You recognize it because you recognize yourself in her.

Those words stole all the breath from his lungs and his chest tightened.

Oh, God.

Davian gaped, first at Cate, then Adella, then Cate again. "I don't… I… How? Why?"

He sounded ridiculous, he knew, but he couldn't seem to wrap his mind around the fact that he had a child. With Cate.

My daughter.

Never once did he doubt Cate's statement. He knew her too well to think her a liar and the timeline worked with what she'd told him earlier about Adella's age. He just… "Why didn't you tell me sooner?"

"I tried to, Davian. I did. As soon as I found out. I got the first positive test a few weeks after you'd left. By then I'd seen the tabloid stories about your engagement and knew the truth of who you were, but I still thought you should know." She sighed and hugged Adella tighter. "I tried to get hold of you, but the school wouldn't give me any of your information. So, I went to the Ruclecian embassy next and explained to them who I was and why I needed to speak with you." Cate snorted. "Looking back now, I can see why they brushed me off as a kook. You must get tons of people claiming to know you, but back then, I was desperate. I even managed to get all the way to one of your security people, but they refused to let me speak with you. Finally, I gave up."

"Cate, I…" For once in his life, Davian was speechless. What could he say to that? He absolutely believed what she said about trying to contact him. And she was right. The tabloids paid big money to people who claimed they knew the royal family of Ruclecia. And kooks abounded, lying about dating the princes or having their babies. Those rules about contacting a member of the royal family were there for a reason. But not for Cate. If there was anyone he'd wanted to talk to back then, it had been her. He'd been too wrapped up in all the scandal and the stress of his father's illness and his fake engagement and he'd never thought…never known…

Davian hung his head, hating how much time they'd lost, how much they'd hurt themselves and each other over the past five years with their estrangement. Then Adella stirred in her mother's arms and blinked her eyes open. Blue. Just like Davian's. And his heart melted completely.

I have a daughter. Adella. My daughter.

Adella sat up and rubbed her eyes, her little mouth pursed. She blinked up at Cate, then over at Davian, her frown increasing. "Who are you? Are you a doctor like Mommy?"

He'd been trained to speak in front of multitudes, to speak with kings and queens and billionaires. But one question from this little girl left him tongue-tied and twisted. Davian stared bug-eyed at his daughter as the gravity of the situation settled in.

Thankfully, Cate intervened by standing, hoisting Adella higher in her arms. "This is Mommy's friend." Davian didn't miss the slight edge on that word. "His name is Dr. de Loroso and you can meet him later, after your nap."

"But I don't want to take a nap, Mommy."

Adella's bottom lip trembled. "I want to stay up here with you and Dr. de Loroso. Please?"

Cate took the whining in stride. "I bet by the time you wake up, François will have the lunch buffet out, and I heard he's going to have fresh pineapple today. That's your favorite, right?"

Adella nodded, still staring over the top of her doll's head at Davian. "Do you like pineapple, Dr. de Loroso?"

Davian swallowed hard against his sandpaper throat and managed to croak out, "Yes. I do."

"Good." Adella grinned and it felt like the sun coming out from behind the clouds to Davian. "We can have pineapple together at lunch then. Right, Mommy?"

Cate looked from their daughter to Davian then back again, wariness still lurking in the shadows of her green eyes. She'd told him the truth about their daughter, but she still didn't trust him with Adella, that much was clear.

Davian didn't know if he trusted himself with Adella. He treated kids in his practice and loved being around them, but he'd never had one of his own. To care for, to raise, to be responsible for. Most days he felt like he barely had enough energy to care for himself and his patients. How was he supposed to ensure the survival of this adorable little girl as well?

But before panic could set in, an odd sense of peace and purpose took over.

Adella is mine. My daughter.

His chest warmed with dedication and determination.

He would do it. Take care of Adella, take care of Cate too. They were his responsibility, and he would not fail. Not now. Not ever.

"Yes," Davian said, pushing to his feet and walking over to them at the top of the stairs. "We'll have pineapple, Adella. I'll make sure of it. Now, go take your nap. I'll see you soon."

To Cate he whispered, "Can we talk more after you put her down?"

She gave a short nod then headed toward the stairs, leaving Davian to watch after them, still coming to grips with the fact that within a matter of minutes he'd gone from a bachelor to a family man with a child and all that implied.

CHAPTER FIVE

BY THE TIME Cate got Adella down for her nap, it was after ten. She carefully closed the cabin door then sagged against the gleaming wood-paneled wall in the hallway and took a deep breath, eyes closed.

What in the world was I thinking, telling Davian about Adella so soon?

Yes, he deserved to know and yes, she'd kept it from him for long enough. But now that the truth was out there, she'd created a whole other boatload of problems. Once she'd discovered he was on board the *Querencia*, she'd planned to observe, see how he was, how things had changed, then ease into the topic when the time was right.

But then there'd been the emergency with Paulo and Davian diving right into why he'd left, and she'd felt vulnerable and open and so why not tell him then. Get it all out in the open.

Except now she was due to meet him in the library, Cate felt oddly protective of her life with

Adella. For five years, it had been just them. Now she had no idea what Davian might ask of her in regard to their daughter and she wasn't sure how to adjust to that.

But if not now, when?

Never one to back down from hard things, Cate steeled herself and pushed away from the wall, and headed upstairs to the library. She'd figure it out. Just like she'd figured out everything else up until now. She entered the yacht's deserted library two minutes later and closed the door behind her. No one usually came here, which was why Cate had suggested this spot for their talk.

Today though, her stomach was full of butterflies and a tremor of adrenaline shook through her bloodstream, keeping her pacing the area instead of settling on one of the comfy seats. She was just about to start straightening the shelves, just to have something to do, when the door opened and in walked Davian.

Lord, he looked good. Nearly the same as he had back in residency. Well, except for the slight hints of silver in the dark hair at his temples. He still had on his black suit, though he'd loosened his tie, she noticed, revealing a tiny vee of tanned throat. She felt a crazy urge to kiss that spot before she clenched her fists at her sides.

Davian closed the door behind him then ran a

hand through his wind-tousled hair, those intense blue eyes searching the room before landing on her in the corner. She'd noticed outside, with everything else going on, but shadows marred the skin beneath his eyes, as if he hadn't been sleeping. Cate knew the feeling. She'd tossed and turned most of the night last night after seeing him again. She found herself wanting to walk over and pull Davian into her arms, let him rest against her for a little while.

Or something.

No. Stop it.

That was the fatigue talking. Back in residency, she'd been used to long hours and little sleep. But years on cruise ships had reset her internal clock. She'd moved past weary some time ago, and if she'd been wise, Cate would've taken a nap right alongside Adella instead of standing here now. But unfortunately, on top of this drama in her personal life, she was also on call today for any medical emergencies that might come up for the clinic, so no rest for her anytime soon. Given that it was just Davian and his parents aboard, they weren't likely to need her, but the crew might. Like poor Juan and Paulo. She made a note to call and check in on him as soon as she and Davian were done talking.

"Hello," Davian said, walking over to take a seat on the sofa. "Am I late?"

"Uh, no. No. You're right on time. Not that this is a formal meeting or anything, I just meant..."

Stop babbling.

Cate started toward the chair across from Davian then halted halfway there, uncertain where to go. Finally, she slipped into the chair across from him and exhaled slowly. "So."

"So."

They watched each other from across the span of the coffee table, but it could've been the Grand Canyon for all the distance between them. The odd intimacy that had surrounded them upstairs on the sundeck earlier had evaporated like the morning fog, leaving nothing but tension in its wake.

"I'm sorry," Davian finally said, frowning down at his hands folded in his lap. "I guess I'm still trying to wrap my head around what you told me earlier. I should be better prepared for this discussion, I suppose, I just..." He threw his hands up. "It's not every day you find out you're a father."

"No, it's not." She almost felt sorry for him. Almost. But she couldn't let herself go there because communication worked both ways and even though she hadn't been able to reach him about the pregnancy, he'd never once tried to check up on her either. Just to make sure she was doing okay, even if he didn't know about the baby. They slept together. That meant something to Cate. But apparently not Davian. So, no. She refused to feel sorry for him now, shoving the traitorous pinch in her chest aside. Summoning her courage, she added, "I don't expect anything from you."

He blinked at her, frowning. "What?"

"For Adella, I mean," Cate clarified. "I only told you about her upstairs because I thought you should know. But I don't need your money or anything. We're doing fine on our own."

Davian shook his head. "I'm sure you are. It's obvious that you're a great mother, Cate. And you're the strongest person I've ever met. I've no doubt you and Adella are doing fine."

"But?"

"But what?"

"You're sure we're doing fine, but…" Cate inhaled deep. "I'm sure there's more to it than that, Davian. You never could leave well enough alone. I remember you running all those extra tests back in residency just to make sure all your i's were dotted and your t's crossed. Even when it drew the ire of our attending. I can't believe you'd do less now when you've just discovered your daughter."

Urgh. *This isn't going well.* Unfortunately, although she did manage to put a halt to her babbling, she couldn't seem to pull her gaze away from Davian and the way he'd unbuttoned his suit coat to show the white shirt beneath. The soft cotton material pulling tighter across his torso to reveal the muscles beneath. Five years might have passed, but if she closed her eyes Cate could still remember the feel of those muscles beneath her fingertips, the warmth of his skin, the scent of soap and spice that clung to his neck, the catch in his breath when her fingers slipped down his abdomen to the waistband of his pants then lower still... She was only human, after all, and it had been so long, too long since she'd been with anyone else. In fact, if she was honest, there hadn't been anyone for her after Davian. What with the pregnancy and her busy work schedule, then later taking care of Adella, there'd been no time for relationships or romance.

"What's she like?" Davian asked quietly, jarring Cate out of her heated thoughts. "What's Adella's favorite color? Her favorite food? When's her birthday? Does she like seafood? Does she have any allergies?" He sat back and shook his head. "I feel like I've missed so much of her life already. I have so much catching up to do." He met Cate's gaze then. "Does she know about me? I mean, about who I am, really?"

Cate bit back a small smile. Davian always did jump in headfirst with things. "She's a typical five-year-old. She constantly asks questions about everything. Her favorite color is pink. Her favorite food is French fries. And pineapple. As you learned earlier. Her birthday is August twelfth. She likes shrimp, crab and lobster, but not so much fish. And no allergies. That I know of yet, anyway." Cate tilted her head slightly. "And no. She only knows you from this morning. I didn't want to say anything to her until an occasion arose when I needed to, like seeing you again. So far, she's never pushed too much for answers about a father, but I suspect that will change soon, what with her starting school when we get back to the States."

"You're going back to the States?" Davian sat forward again.

"Yes, after this charter. It's time we settled down so Adella can get some roots and grow up in one spot." Cate realized this was the first time she'd talked to anyone about her plans, other than Dr. Bryant and her mother back in Boston. "And I've saved up enough now to start my own practice, so that's what I'm going to do."

"Wow, congratulations." Davian's tone held a bit of awe. "I wondered what happened to your old dreams."

"Still alive and well, thanks." She hesitated a moment, wondering how much to share with him, then thought what the hell. Might as well put it all on the table now. Save time later. "I have the property picked out and everything. All I need to do is make a down payment and hire the construction company."

"In Boston, then? Where you grew up?"

"No. California." She brushed nonexistent lint from the front of her shirt. "Near Salinas. There's a huge migrant population in that area and I want to help them get affordable medical care."

Davian smiled then and Cate's pulse stumbled like a drunken sailor. "Always the idealist, eh?"

"Always." She ignored the thrill of having his full attention on her again and switched the spotlight back to him. "What about you? You said you run a hospital in Ruclecia? Wouldn't have taken you for an administrator. You always loved surgery so much."

"Still do," he said, his face lighting up as he talked shop with her. "I've hired people to help with the administrative aspects. You're right. I don't like that part. Too much paperwork and red tape. I do the hands-on work. And I teach. I've been giving seminars on new advancements in lasers for general surgery for the last year or so. Patients are still my top priority."

"Well, it sounds like we both got what we wanted then," Cate said.

"Not everything, no."

The flicker of hurt and loneliness in his eyes made her chest squeeze tight. If Cate was honest, she'd not gotten everything she wanted either. The one thing that had gotten away sat across from her now, as far out of her reach as he'd ever been, single or not. She'd opened up to him, told him things she'd never told anyone else—about her past, about her father, about her dreams for the future. She'd felt closer to him than anyone else on earth. She'd thought they'd find happily ever after together and ride off into the sunset. But then his lies had been revealed. He wasn't who he'd pretended to be. He wasn't trustworthy. He'd trampled on her heart just like her father had done. Even worse, he was royalty. He was wealthy and worldly and had duties and responsibilities far beyond what Cate would ever know. There was no way they could be together now, even with a daughter between them.

Not that she was thinking of being with Davian again. She wasn't. It was the tiredness talking.

That was the excuse she was going with anyway.

Nothing but fantasies about what might have been. That was normal, right? Wishing and wondering.

They stared at each other again, until Davian shifted his weight in his seat and crossed his legs to mirror hers. "Look, do you think we could start over, Cate?" he asked. "We kind of got off on the wrong foot yesterday, I think."

"That might be because you disappeared five years ago into thin air," Cate said pointedly.

His gaze darted to the other side of the room. "Yes, there is that I suppose."

It was still odd to hear him admit it so freely, even after their conversation on the sundeck. But he'd told her the details of his hasty departure and it was all in the past now anyway. No way to change it. Still, she wanted to make sure it wouldn't happen again, with Adella. "Look, you haven't said what your intentions are regarding Adella, or even if you intend to tell her that you're her father, but I feel I must set some ground rules for you, as her mother. And I want to be clear up front. If you're planning to disappear again without a word, then I think it's best if we just leave things as they are right now. She can learn more about you and her heritage later when she'll understand better."

For a moment, it looked like Davian would argue. But then he sighed and gave a curt nod. "Agreed. But for the record, I do not plan to disappear again. I never meant to disappear at all. But my duties demanded—"

"If we tell Adella who you are, then you have a duty to her as well," Cate said, not budging an inch. "Better she has no father at all than to have one that vanishes from her life without a trace. I know what that feels like, and I won't put my daughter through that ever."

"I'll be there for her, Cate. I promise." He sighed and hung his head. "I know how difficult this is for you. After what you went through with your own father. And I know that I went and did the same..." He threw up his hands and looked away. "I'm sorrier about that than I can ever say. I screwed up and I know it. And all I can do now is beg your forgiveness and say that no matter what else happens, I will never disappear on you and Adella again."

She wanted to believe him, so much her heart ached, but she couldn't. Not yet. Not until he'd proven himself worthy. She'd trusted him once and it had nearly broken her. She uncrossed then recrossed her legs the opposite direction, wincing at the needle pricks through her nerve endings as the blood began to circulate to her lower extremities again.

"Perhaps you could come to dinner one night," Davian said, sounding exhausted. "Here on the yacht. My parents would be there..."

"No," she said, meeting his gaze again. "Not until we've talked to Adella and worked out how all of this will work. I don't want to confuse her by having her meet grandparents."

"Okay." He nodded. "I get that. Maybe we

could go ashore at our next stop. Spend a day together, get to know each other then maybe we can tell her the truth about who I am." Davian cleared his throat. "I mean, if it feels right and all."

Cate wasn't sure what she'd expected of this conversation, but this wasn't it. The fact Davian was being so gracious and accepting of it all set her warning bells on high alert. She wasn't used to things going so smoothly. Even Cate had to admit though that his excursion plan sounded like a good idea. "Okay," she said at last. "But I'll need to check my schedule at the clinic and make sure I have the day off. I'll let you know."

There was still one question though that lingered in her mind.

"Why haven't you asked for paternity tests?" Cate asked bluntly.

Davian chuckled. "Because I know that once my parents find out, all of that will be done. Royal succession and all. But for now, it's only you and I that know, and I trust you, Cate. I always have."

Now it was her turn to be speechless. For all the faults and foibles they'd had back in residency, trust wasn't one of them. At least until he'd left her high and dry, that was. The fact he still trusted her now though…well, that was something, wasn't it?

"Right." Davian stood then and walked to the door. "I need to get back to my parents. They've been raving about some tour of Monte Carlo they want to take when we get to Monaco, and I need to make sure everything is set up properly and security is in place for them."

Cate stood too and followed him out of the library. "Don't you have people for that?"

He snorted. "I'm the spare to the heir, Cate. I'm all the 'people' they need."

The twinge of resignation in his voice made her sympathize for him, despite her wishes. "I'm sorry. It must be hard to be treated like a servant in your own household."

"I'm used to it," he said. "It's been that way since I was a boy, so I've learned to work within it. And really, I don't have it so hard. I'm privileged and I know it. No reason to feel sorry for myself. A lot of other people have it much, much worse and I know it. So, I've made it my mission in life to help them as much as I can, through my medical work and through the charities I support. Hopefully, I'm doing so."

Back in residency, Cate had been drawn to him because of their shared vision and ideals, and the pull was no less strong now, even all these years later. As she turned to head back to the clinic as he went the opposite way down the hall to go above decks, Cate said, "I think you are, from what you've told me." Their gazes held for a beat or two, until the warmth of awareness sizzling between them grew too hot to ignore. Rather than deal with that though, Cate inched back down the hall toward the safety of her clinic. "I'll let you know my schedule for Monaco."

"Cate?" Davian called just as she reached the clinic door. He waited until she turned back to him to say, "Thank you."

A long moment passed after he was gone before Cate moved again, an odd mix of anticipation and apprehension bubbling inside her. She'd just made either the best or worst decision of her life. Only time would tell.

CHAPTER SIX

ONCE THE SHOCK of knowing he had a daughter wore off for Davian, he began to realize that keeping Adella sheltered from the truth of her heritage might not be so simple after all. Especially with his nosy parents watching him like a hawk every second of the cruise. God. What an absolute mess he'd made of all this. And whether that had been his decision or intention or not, it was up to him to clean it up now and deal with the consequences of his actions back then.

A daughter. I have a daughter.

Those words still filled him with an odd mix of elation and apprehension. He'd always wanted children, a family of his own, but had thought he'd have more time to plan and prepare. The last thing he wanted to do was bring a child of his into the turmoil of royalty, but the reality was he didn't have much choice in the matter now. Adella was his and as such he would protect her with his own life against any foe, even his own family, if necessary. They'd already cost him too much in his life. A relationship with his own daughter would not be another casualty of his duties. He refused to let that happen.

"What is wrong with you, my son?" Davian's father, King Phillipe, said the next morning over breakfast. "You seem distracted. And your expression is as fierce as a tiger."

"I'm fine," Davian mumbled, sipping more of his coffee and scowling.

The crew of the *Querencia* had laid out a fine feast for the first meal of the day, but Davian didn't have much appetite. The same did not seem to be an issue for his parents and their guests. Besides King Phillipe and Davian's mother, Queen Arabella, they'd invited a small cohort of their most trusted friends and advisors to come along on this trip, both as a reward for years of loyal service and to keep his parents from getting bored while sailing between destinations, and allowing Davian time to do other things besides entertaining them. At first, he'd figured he'd spend most of the time in his cabin, preparing notes and lecture materials for another medical conference coming up the following month where Davian was presenting on a new medical technology in the operating room to three-dimensionally print implants to perfectly match the patient's needs at the time of surgery.

Normally, he'd be doing all of this at home, in his private villa. But he and his older brother had discussed the rising threats against his parents and decided it was best to separate the current King from the Crown Prince for a while, and because Davian's work was more portable, he'd gotten the job of babysitting his parents on this cruise. He took a deep breath and stared down at his notes again. It was all incredibly fascinating and state-of-the-art medicine that Davian hoped to bring to his teaching hospital and the people of Ruclecia soon. But for now, instead, he was torn between preparations for his presentation and spending more time with Cate and Adella.

"Are you hungry, sweetheart?" his mother asked from beside Davian at the table. "You should eat a little something at least. Keep your strength up."

Davian gave his mother a small smile and served himself up some fresh fruit from the nearby platter in front of him, then also took a freshly made croissant, still warm from the oven, and added it to his plate.

"Have you planned out our agenda yet for Monte Carlo?" his mother asked. "Please don't forget to coordinate with Marco at the hotel. He knows exactly what we want to see on our tour this week."

"Yes." King Phillipe sat back with a sigh. "It's

too bad your brother couldn't be here as well. He loves Monte Carlo so."

The reason he's not here is to keep you safe, Davian wanted to say, but bit back the response. Fighting with his father over an issue that had long since been settled would do him no good. Best to just let it slide off him and get on with his day. He had more important things to think about now.

Like Cate and his daughter.

Adella.

While he'd never cared for the wealth and privileges his royal status provided, his daughter deserved to at least have access to those benefits until she was old enough to choose on her own. Davian could provide that for her, once all the paternity tests were completed and the results confirmed. Not that there'd been a second when he'd doubted Cate's word about Adella. He believed Cate. Trusted her. He always had. But once Adella's identity was confirmed, then a whole new set of issues would arise. He worried she would also become a target for the extremist threats. Having Cate and their daughter back in his life meant they would be involved now too. And that was why he couldn't let his feelings get the better of him. He had to remain rational, logical, as he figured all this out.

Davian exhaled slowly and scrubbed a hand

over his face, sinking back into the cushions of the sofa he sat on. It was all so complex and complicated.

He walked up to the upper sundeck and stared out over the turquoise waters of the Mediterranean. It was about nine thirty now and the sun was rising. Blue skies above as far as the eye could see and already the sea was busy. Smaller vessels sailed alongside huge cargo ships, delivering goods from all over the globe. A slight breeze blew as they cut through the water, their captain steering them deftly through the traffic and out into the less crowded areas. Perhaps, if he'd not become a doctor, Davian would've joined the royal Ruclecian navy. He loved the water and loved sailing.

From somewhere down below, he heard a familiar chuckle dancing through the air like wind chimes and a sizzle of awareness went through him once more, same as it always did when she was close to him.

Cate.

Even after all these years, the attraction was still there, stronger than ever. Even more so now that he knew what she'd gone through without him. Carrying his baby, alone. Completing residency without him as he'd completed his own back in Ruclecia. Making a life for herself and Adella, on her own, as he'd taken over the hospital in his homeland and begun to build it into the powerhouse, world-renowned medical center it was today.

She'd been through so much already, before they'd met, then he'd put her through so much more. Not intentionally, but that meant little now. Cate's life had been totally disrupted after he'd left. And while she'd managed to bounce back from it all admirably, he still wanted to take care of Cate too. For all they once meant to each other and because she was Adella's mother.

The only trouble was, he would need to keep all of it—and them—out of the public eye. Not because he was embarrassed by them, but for their own protection. They had no idea what he and his family went through daily, hounded by the paparazzi whenever they went out. Not to mention the threats and security scares that had driven them to take this cruise now. Davian wanted none of that sordidness to touch Cate and Adella.

What they had, his past with Cate, and his future with Adella, was all too personal, too precious to him, especially now he'd just rediscovered Cate and found out for the first time about Adella. Davian never wanted them to be in danger because of who he was or what he had.

He stood there for a long time, staring out to sea and thinking. His chest ached at the thought of the press hounding his little girl as they'd done to Davian his whole life. The constant sting of feeling vulnerable, of being used and hurt and betrayed by those closest to you for their own devices were wounds he'd carried with him daily and Davian vowed now to do what he must to protect Cate and their daughter from the speculation, the rumors, the constant threats—especially if he wasn't there to protect them personally.

Dammit.

He removed his sunglasses and scrubbed a hand over his face, before replacing his shades. He needed to concentrate on the security for his parents' upcoming tour of Monte Carlo and his presentation, not Cate. And yet, he couldn't seem to stop himself. He glanced at his watch and realized he'd been up here fifteen minutes now and he needed to get a move on.

He had phone calls to make, a man named Marco to locate and speak with about his parents' "special" tours, then security staff to brief on the agenda. He also needed to make sure all the paperwork and IDs were in place for customs ahead of time to make sure his parents would not be stopped or detained in any way. A day of leisure for the royals made possible by Davian's day of hard work and frustration. If things went as they were supposed to.

If...

And yet more proof that Davian was more of a highly decorated secretary than a prince.

He missed his patients and his hospital. Yet here he was, fulfilling his duties again instead of fulfilling his passions in life. He'd stuck with his family this long out of a sense of obligation, a sense of loyalty. He'd admired his grandfather, loved his parents and brother too—even if he didn't always understand or agree with their motivations. And after the debacle with Cate, he'd honestly not had much else going on with his life other than his work, thinking he'd throw himself into medicine and let the rest play out without him. But then the threats had increased and he'd been called into service for king and crown again.

When he and his brother had originally planned this impromptu trip for the King and Queen, it was meant to be a quiet recuperation period for their father and mother, a way to keep them safe and out of the public eye until the would-be assassins were captured. But with their father loving the spotlight and pomp his position afforded, keeping King Phillipe from his adoring public was like trying to keep sand from slipping through your fingers. Davian sighed and stared out at the horizon, rocky cliffs dotted with pastel houses and white umbrellas. Sometimes it felt like even with all his careful planning and work, they were all doomed.

Davian quickly shoved aside those thoughts though. Feeling sorry for himself was not his nature. Action was, and he had plenty of work to keep him busy. He went back downstairs to his stateroom and began preparing for the Monte Carlo visit. He talked to the infamous Marco and was assured the tour was taken care of. Then he'd sat down and gone through all the tabloids he'd asked Chief Stew Noah to deliver to him earlier. Thankfully, there was no sign of any stories about their trip aboard the *Querencia*. After going through the papers and the websites on the internet, he called his hospital back in Ruclecia to check on his patients. So far, so good.

By the time he was done with his calls and his work, it was late afternoon. Davian went back up on deck to stretch his legs and get some fresh air. He walked to the aft deck and stood watching the waves made by the *Querencia*'s powerful engines as she sliced through the sea, pushing them onward toward Monaco and the future. He turned to rest his elbows on the shiny metal railing when he spotted Cate, standing on the forward starboard bow, her blond hair blowing in the breeze and her eyes closed, as if she were making a wish or dreaming. She wasn't wearing her medical uniform today. Instead, she was in a white polo shirt and shorts, her long tan legs and bare feet making his throat constrict with sudden want. He remembered those legs, how soft and smooth they'd felt beneath his hands, how strong they were wrapped around his waist as he'd driven them both to the edge of ecstasy inside her…

Adella wasn't around, that he could see, and Davian found himself wanting to walk up there, to pull her into his arms and kiss her, run his hands through her silky hair and tangle his fingers in it as he tipped her head back to lick the pulse point at the base of her neck, the one that made her gasp and whimper when he nipped it gently just so.

His body tightened and Davian suddenly felt way too overdressed in his cream linen suit and ivory dress shirt, the aqua silk tie he'd chosen in homage to the sea. He wanted to strip then and there. Put on comfortable clothes like hers and…

Cate turned slightly then and saw him down the length of the ship. Davian took an involuntary step forward and Cate took one back. Of their own accord, his feet led him toward her. But the nearer Davian drew to Cate, the farther away she seemed to move, until she backed herself right into the railing behind her.

"How are you this morning?" Davian asked past his tight vocal cords, doing his best to sound casual as he came to a halt beside Cate. "You look lovely today."

Alone with Cate, a bit of awkwardness kicked in again. He'd called her lovely, but it paled in comparison to her true beauty. She was the loveliest person, inside and out, he'd ever seen, but that wasn't something you just walked up and said to a person, right? Especially after five years apart and the history they'd had.

Still, Cate blushed under his words and gripped the railing more tightly, lowering her head. He couldn't see her eyes behind those dark sunglasses she wore, but Davian got the sense—as he always had—that Cate was uncomfortable with praise, simple or not. As if she was unused to receiving it. She'd talked to him briefly back in residency about her childhood, being raised by a single mother after her father left them when Cate was ten. At the time, she'd brushed over it so swiftly that Davian had assumed she'd bounced back from the pain of it quickly and resiliently. But now, considering what he knew about her and what he was observing today, he had to wonder if that experience hadn't left deeper scars that were still affecting Cate today. Especially since her demeanor suggested she had no idea how to react to receiving a compliment.

"Uh, thanks," Cate said, still looking downward, her tone edged with discomfort. "When we're not working aboard ship, we dress down in our casual uniforms. They're supplied by the yacht owners, so we don't have much choice in color or style," Cate hastened to add.

The fact she was babbling, as if nervous, helped lessen the tension inside Davian. He wasn't the only one scared of messing this up then. That was reassuring. Because given how much he wanted this reunion with Cate to go well, it felt like all his years of elocution training had gone right out the window and he might start babbling himself soon too.

Instead, he cleared his throat and took a deep breath before saying, "No, can't go wrong there."

They stood staring out to sea again, shoulder to shoulder at the railing. Every so often, Davian's arm would brush against Cate's and a frisson of need would race through him like a Formula 1 car, prompting new images of Cate in a tiny bikini and nothing else to flash in his mind. His traitorous body went into overdrive again—heart racing, blood thumping in his ears, chest constricted, and pants suddenly too tight for comfort. Thank goodness for his suit coat to cover his reactions or he'd embarrass himself. Davian squeezed his eyes shut and battled for control. He wasn't some schoolboy virgin. He had years of experience with beautiful women. He shouldn't be this way just standing next to

Cate—fumbling and frustrated and fantastically turned on—and yet, he was.

God help me.

"So, I checked the clinic schedule for our arrival in Monaco in a couple days' time," Cate said. "And I should be able to go into Monte Carlo during the day, as Dr. Bryant is on call then. But I'll need to be back that night to take over from him."

"Great," Davian said, wondering when the temperature here had gotten so hot.

They stood side by side again in silence. Davian didn't know about Cate's nervousness, but his own was still there, just beneath the surface, ready to trickle out and ruin any cool confidence he might have projected up to this point, so he kept quiet again.

"Anyway," Cate said after a while. "I told Adella that we'd be going ashore, and she was super excited. She was asking me all about Monaco and I told her as much as I could, but I'm hoping you'll know more about it, being—" she waved a hand over him "—a prince and all." Her cheeks pinked adorably again. "I mean, not that you spend all your time there or anything. Obviously, you don't. Or you didn't, because you went to medical school and everything, so that was four years right there. Then residency, which was another four years. And a fellowship that took another three. So, eleven years you spent not going to Monaco."

Davian let her finish, biting back a smile. "Yes. Thanks for the rundown of my schooling thus far."

Even with the sunglasses in place, he could imagine those green eyes of hers widening with mortification. Cate cursed under her breath then shook her head. "Sorry. I don't know why I'm so nervous. It's not like we haven't talked before or anything. Hell, we did a lot more than talk—" She stopped abruptly. "Sorry. God, just stop talking already, Cate."

Davian did smile then, shoving his hands in his pockets to keep from reaching for her. She looked so adorably ruffled he just wanted to hug her and tell her everything would be fine, even if it wouldn't. "It's okay. I understand, Cate. I do. And you make me nervous too. I think maybe it's just been a while and we're both trying to be careful not to screw this up, yeah?"

She inhaled deep and grinned back at him and his world went supernova bright, like the difference between regular color and Technicolor brilliance. "Yeah. You're right. Maybe we're putting too much pressure on ourselves."

"Maybe we are." Davian rocked back on his heels, searching for a new, safer topic of conversation. "Have you gotten any updates on Paulo?"

"Yes," Cate said, shifting her weight to lean a hip against the railing. "He's doing much better. I spoke to his father, and he said they should be releasing his son later today. He had a concussion, but no fracture, thank goodness. They should be rejoining us on board the *Querencia* in Monaco."

"Excellent."

"What about your parents?" Cate asked, tilting her head slightly. "Aren't they going into Monte Carlo too? I heard Noah talking to the crew about it this morning in the cafeteria. They're making plans for a big picnic lunch and everything for the guests."

"Yes, they're going ashore too. Not with us though," Davian added. "I spent the better part of my day today making sure everything was set and security would be in place for their visit."

She studied him for along moment, then frowned. "You don't look happy about it."

"I'm just concerned, that's all."

"About their safety?"

"Yes. There've been threats back in Ruclecia."

"Threats?" Cate's frown deepened. "What kind of threats?"

"Of assassination. Like what happened to my grandfather." Davian leaned his elbows on the railing then, glad for the cool sea breeze on his heated face. He hung his head and took a deep breath as the old grief dissolved. "The original group of fringe radicals responsible for my grandfather's death were locked away for life years ago. But now a new group has resurfaced and are demanding an end to the monarchy in my country. They're a small but vocal minority. My father, King Phillipe, has done well though for the people of Ruclecia and most of our citizens want my family to remain in power. Of course, my father's recent heart attack didn't help, nor did his quadruple bypass surgery. He's in his late sixties now and ready to step down. He wants to turn things over to my older brother, Crown Prince Arthur, and let him lead Ruclecia into the future, but it's risky at present with all these new threats and his health concerns. The last thing we want is to start a revolution or damage the people's faith in our monarchy. So, my brother and I decided, along with our security team, that the best thing at this point was to get our parents out of the country for a while. Let him rest and recuperate while Arthur takes the reins temporarily to prove he can do it. Let the anger and outrage of the fringe calm a bit. Then we'll go back home and see where things stand."

"Wow." The sun disappeared behind a cloud and Cate lifted her sunglasses, allowing him to see her gorgeous green eyes. Davian did the same with his own glasses, letting them rest atop his head.

They watched each other for a beat or two, before Cate crossed her arms and stared down at her bare toes on the deck. Her toenails were painted pink, Davian noticed. His mind then imagined him kissing each of her cute toes and making her giggle then gasp with need, which wasn't helpful at all.

Oh, boy.

Cate must've been able to read his thoughts because her gaze flicked down to his lips, her own mouth going a little slack as her green eyes darkened slightly. His pulse tripped at the idea that maybe he wasn't the only one struggling to keep his reactions hidden. The atmosphere between them seemed to crackle with energy and if he leaned in, just a few inches, he could kiss her. See for himself if it was as wonderful as he remembered. See if she tasted as sweet as she had five years ago or…

Stop. Focus.

"So, Monaco," Cate said a short while later, her voice a tad breathless as he turned to face the sea again and slid her sunglasses back into place and the sun blazed once more.

"Yes, Monaco," he responded, for lack of anything better. "It's nice there. Have you been before?"

Now it was her turn to snort. "God, no. Telegraph Hill, Boston," Cate said, laying on her accent thick. "I'm a Southie through and through. Never imagined Monaco in my future."

Davian understood that, though in a slightly different way. Growing up in the palace in Ruclecia, he'd never imagined having the chance to go to live in America, to attend medical school there, to meet a woman as wonderful as Cate. But even back then, he'd dreamed of getting out, of living a real life, a true life, helping people. Part of that had to do with his grandfather's assassination, as he'd told her, but the other part was just born into him, he supposed. The need for more than just an existence of pampered perfection where life was kept a safe distance away and nothing ever changed. Maybe that was what Cate had felt growing up too. Not the pampered perfection part, obviously, but the need to forge a new path, to escape the monotony, to create your own destiny.

"Was it terrible, growing up where you did?" Davian asked.

"No. Not terrible. Just not…" Cate shrugged. "Not what I wanted. So, I left home and struck out on my own."

"When you went to medical school?"

"Yep. Not that I went far. Just across town. I got a cheap apartment with three other girls off campus, and we all worked waitress jobs to pay the bills while we were in school. My financial aid covered classes and books and stuff, but not room and board."

"And you still graduated top of your class."

"Damn straight I did." Cate grinned. She lifted her face to the sun and Davian couldn't help tracking the line of her long, tanned throat before he forced his gaze elsewhere. When she finally looked at him again, Cate asked him, "What about you? You must love being home in Ruclecia again."

"Hmm." He did love his homeland. Always would. But lately, he couldn't help feeling there was something missing. Or more precisely, someone. Someone to share his life with, someone to make a home with. "Ruclecia is very beautiful, but so was California. I guess I'm still searching for my true home. The place where I fit in the most. I feel that at work, at my hospital. I know I'm doing good there."

"But not at the palace," she said, turning to mimic his stance, leaning her elbows on the railing beside his.

"No, not at the palace."

Cate nodded. "I'm glad you know about Adella now. But if you hurt her, Davian, you will have to deal with me. Understand?"

"I won't hurt her," he said. "I swear." At Cate's

raised brow, he added, "I swear I'll do my very best never to hurt her. There are no guarantees in life, but I promise, on my honor, to never intentionally do anything to cause her pain in any way. All right?"

"All right." Cate gave a curt nod then straightened. "I should probably get back to the clinic. Lots of stocking to do."

Davian straightened as well. "I'll keep planning our day in Monaco. It's your first time and I want it to be special. For you and for Adella."

"Sounds good."

As Davian watched Cate walk away down the stairs, a strange sense of gravity came over him. This moment felt huge, even though it was such a small thing. A conversation between two people, and yet, he'd never felt anything quite like it in his life. So full of potential and promise and possibilities. This day would be important, in ways he could only imagine, and he doubted he'd ever get another chance like it again, so he wanted to make the most of the opportunity and make their day in Monaco as a family as amazing as he could for all of them.

Cate went back downstairs to the clinic and began helping Carrie, the clinic's second crew member and receptionist, restock the supply cabinets. After the first two days of the charter, there hadn't been much for them to do on board, though with the King's heart condition Davian wanted a trained physician on call 24/7, so...

Davian. David.

No matter what name he went by, her body would still recognize him a mile away.

Hard to believe that even after all that had happened between them, that same awareness, that same heightened attraction was still there. At least for her. And after catching Davian looking at her like he wanted to devour her whole, Cate thought it was for him too.

Not that they'd act on it.

Been there, done that. Had the scars to prove it.

But still, a girl could dream.

And speaking of dreams...

"And did you see the pictures of their palace in the latest issue of *Royal Life*?" Carrie asked as she stuffed another handful of alcohol wipes into a bin on the shelf. "Talk about opulence. I think one rug alone in that place costs more than the entire house I grew up in."

Cate wasn't really paying attention though, her mind focused on the man upstairs, who'd told her about his past and seeing his grandfather assassinated before his eyes and how that made him want to be a doctor. She could see that now, in how dedicated he was to his patients, in his need to give back and help others. In his desire to serve instead of being served. Another reason, she supposed, why he'd put up with all the royal intrigue and disruptions to his life thus far. His innate sense of needing to be helpful. A trait he'd shown her so many times during their residency together.

When Davian had walked out of her life five years ago, Cate had convinced herself that all the stories and rumors of the playboy prince who only cared for himself were true. Given how angry and betrayed she'd felt because of his lies, hearing about all his awful deeds confirmed she didn't need him in her life. That him leaving was the best thing that could have happened to her.

Then she'd found out she was pregnant, and the world had dropped out from under her.

And the fact he hadn't responded when she tried to reach out, well that was more than enough reason for Cate to go it alone.

But now, she was exhausted. Raising a child with limited support and crazy doctor's hours was far more difficult than she'd realized. Her mother helped some, when she could, but Cate needed more.

Davian could give you more.

And she had to think of Adella's future too. Ruclecia and its royal family were a part of her birthright. She deserved to know them and what she'd be giving up, but not until she was older and could make her own choice. Which left Cate in charge until then.

"Okay. Let's do the tongue depressors next," Carrie said, walking over to grab another box from the stack against the wall. They brought aboard fresh provisions at their last stop at Marseille last night, so there was quite a bit of stuff to put away. Carrie opened the top of the box and set it between her and Cate on the counter before grabbing a clear glass jar from the row of them against the wall on the countertop and began to fill it with the wooden sticks. "So, what do you think of Prince Davian? Pretty hot, huh?"

Cate scowled, feeling oddly protective of him. "How would you know?"

"I met him yesterday," Carrie said, grinning. "When he came to the clinic looking for you. Lucky girl. How did you meet him?"

Not sure how to answer that without getting into a whole thing, Cate grabbed a huge handful of tongue depressors and shoved them into the jar, then got up and went over to look through the other boxes, still aware of Carrie's stare following her around the room.

"Oh, uh…" Cate grabbed a box of paper gowns and bent to fill the drawer below the exam table. "We met in passing at a medical conference one year in California. Barely know the guy. Not sure why he'd come looking for me now."

"Really?" Rather than taking the hint of Cate's less than enthusiastic tone that she didn't want to discuss this anymore, Carrie straightened and gave Cate an inquiring look. "That's weird, because I swear I overheard Dr. Bryant talking to him like you two were old friends."

"What?" Cate tensed up then forced herself to relax. "Seriously. I've no idea what Dr. Bryant was talking about." Then just to drive home her point, Cate looked up at her coworker over the exam table with a pointed stare.

The assistant sighed and turned back around to shove the rest of the tongue depressors into the jar. Thankfully, they worked in companionable silence after that, getting everything ready in case the guests needed medical attention while aboard the yacht.

So, what do you think of Prince Davian? Pretty hot, huh?

Still, Carrie's question kept looping around in Cate's mind. Yes, Davian was hot, regardless of how much she might want to pretend otherwise. In fact, spending time with him up on deck earlier had been nice. Better than nice if she was honest. It reminded her of the easy camaraderie they'd always shared working together back in residency. They seemed to know each other's thoughts and actions before they even knew themselves. Weird, that.

And then there'd been that look.

The one there when they'd been at the railing, where Davian's blue eyes had lit with fire and hunger as he'd stared at her mouth, making her lips tingle even if he'd never kissed her today. Made her remember what it had been like all those years ago between them. She'd had to grip the railing tight just to keep from reaching for him then, to keep from throwing him down on the deck and having her wicked way with him over and over again.

Which made no sense. They were different people now than they'd been five years ago, and she doubted that even with a child between them she'd be the kind of woman Davian wanted or needed in his life. She was too busy, too focused on her work and her and Adella's futures.

Davian, even though he didn't really claim the title, was still a prince. The son of a king. An accomplished doctor and surgeon in his own right. He could rent boats like the *Querencia* to just sail around on for two weeks. He could jet off to the other side of the world on a private jet whenever he liked. Why would he want a plain old GP like Cate Neves who planned to set up a neighborhood clinic when she was done with this charter and leave her yachting life behind for their daughter's schooling?

It made no sense. And yes, there was Adella, but couples coparented all the time now and lived in different countries while doing it. There was no reason they had to spend time together after this charter. And yet, a deep ache of loneliness inside her said that Cate still wanted him to want that, the same as she did.

Silly, but still there regardless.

And going into Monaco with him in a couple of days won't make that any easier to deny...

True. But it was too late to back out now. In fact, not going would probably look even more conspicuous than going, so yeah. Cate was stuck with that decision. She could do it. She'd be fine. And they'd have Adella there as a buffer. Adella, who never stopped asking questions about everything could carry a conversation all by herself if Cate let her. No need to worry about those awkward silences between her and Davian. Nope. Or those steamy stares that made her heart race and her body throb. Hard to get your groove on with a talkative, nosy kid around all day.

Maybe it wouldn't be so bad after all. Cate was excited to see Monte Carlo, so...

Besides, Davian hadn't once done anything earlier to back up those heated glances of his, so maybe she'd been mistaken about his intentions, or made it up entirely in her own head.

Then she pictured him up on deck, sunlight bathing him, windblown and way too handsome for his own good in his suit and tie. Cate chuckled. Only Davian could get away with wearing a suit and tie at sea and not look like a pompous ass. She hadn't missed the fact that the shade of his blue tie had perfectly matched his eyes either. For an odd second, Cate remembered that Grace Kelly had become Princess of Monaco and wondered what it might be like to marry a man like Davian.

Then she quickly snapped out of it. This wasn't some Hollywood fairy tale and Davian wasn't her Prince Charming to sweep Cate and Adella away to his castle to live happily ever after. At best, they'd have one full day together, to get to know one another better and build a bond that would have to last them for years or longer. Because once Adella was in school, Cate didn't want to move her around too much, so if Davian wanted to see her, he'd have to travel to America. Or maybe she and Adella could go see him in Ruclecia during the summer break. But then Cate would have her clinic and it might be difficult to get away then too and…

"Cate?" Carrie asked. "Did you hear me?"

Nope. She hadn't. Heat prickled her cheeks

as Cate glanced over at the young receptionist. "Sorry. I didn't."

"Everything okay?"

"Fine. Thanks." She swiped the back of her hand over her forehead. "Just tired. Sorry. What was your question again?"

"No question." Carrie gave her a curious look. "Just said my shift's over now. I'll see you tomorrow."

"Yes, see you tomorrow," Cate said. "I have the day off after that but I'll be back on Thursday."

"That's right." Carrie grinned and pointed to the calendar on her desk out front. "See you tomorrow then."

"Thanks. Enjoy your night."

Once she was alone, Cate finished with the last few boxes of supplies and broke down the boxes for recycling, then locked up the clinic for the night. She made sure the yacht's walkie-talkie was still clipped to the back waistband of her shorts in case there was an emergency, then checked her watch. Almost dinnertime. If she hurried, she might be able to grab a plate of food to take out on the deck by the anchors to watch the sunset with Noah and Adella.

Francois had outdone himself again with the galley fare for the crew. There was grilled shrimp and roasted veggies. Rice and homemade French fries. Even some leftover crab and lobster tails from the lunch buffet for the royals. She loaded up a plate with enough food for all three of them to enjoy, then headed upstairs to the front of the ship. They were sailing west, and the sky was clear, so the view of the sunset should be spectacular tonight.

Except when she got close to the bow, the male voice she heard with Adella wasn't the one she expected.

Davian. What the—?

She hurried to the bow and stopped short at the sight of Davian and their daughter. He was pointing out different spots on the shoreline and Adella seemed completely enraptured in his voice. For a brief second, panic welled inside her because she realized everything was changing. Then she quickly got herself back under control, forcing her feelings down deep where they belonged.

Of course he should spend time with Adella. She was his daughter. No need to worry.

Nope.

Cate still worried deep inside. Rather than voicing that though, she asked instead, "Where's Noah?"

Davian looked up, his cheeks pink from the wind and damn if Cate's heart didn't melt a little more. His smile, even and white in his tanned face, didn't help either. "He went inside to change."

"And eat," Adella added, looking over at Cate for the first time. Or rather, the plate of food in her hand. "Is that for me, Mommy? I'm starving."

"Yes," Cate said, her gaze still locked with Davian's. "I mean, yes. It's dinner. I brought enough for you and I and Noah, but if he's not here then—"

"I guess I'll just have to take his place," Davian volunteered, eyeing the lobster tails on the plate Cate held. "The seafood on board is excellent."

Flustered, Cate set the food and napkins on a small table Noah had set up earlier, then pulled out the bottles of water she'd stuck in her shorts pockets to carry them up here. "Uh, yeah. They catch it all locally. The seafood, I mean. The chef buys it right off the boats each morning. Can't get any fresher than that."

She helped Adella into one of the seats and got her situated with a bottle of water, a napkin tucked into the collar of her shirt like a bib, and some shrimp and fries. Then she picked up a lobster tail and perched atop one of the shiny silver windlasses used to raise and lower the anchors, since there were only two chairs to sit on to eat. Davian picked up a lobster tail as well and took a huge bite of the meat before looking up and catching her watching him with amusement. Butter slicked his mouth and he looked like a guilty schoolboy caught with his hand in the cookie jar. So, basically adorable. And handsome. And sexy. And enticing. And…

"Should you be sitting on that?" Davian asked, indicating the windlass with his non-lobster-holding hand.

"He's right, Mommy. Noah told me to never touch those things," Adella added.

"Oh, well." Cate stood and moved over to the table again. "I think he meant that kids shouldn't touch them, but adults are okay."

"I want to be an adult," Adella said, pouting. "You guys get to do all the fun stuff."

Cate and Davian locked eyes, both obviously fighting smiles, before Davian reached over to ruffle his daughter's hair. "Don't rush it, kid. Take your time. Enjoy being a kid."

"That's what everyone always says." Adella sighed, then brightened as she looked up at Cate. "Mommy, do you know Davian? He's my new friend. He knows all about the g'ography here."

"Uh, yes. I met Davian before," she said, giving him a warning look. "And I think you mean geography. That's the study of land."

"That's what I said." Adella giggled, then tried

to feed her stuffed monkey a chip. "Are we going to watch the sunset, Mommy?"

"That's the plan." Cate took another bite of lobster. Sweet and salty goodness.

"Mind if I join you?" Davian asked quietly, probably to avoid Adella hearing him.

Unfortunately, what he wasn't familiar with was a five-year-old's bat-like sonar. When it was something she cared about, Adella could hear things a whole ship-length away. Now, if she was trying to ignore you, then it was another story.

"Oh, Mommy!" Adella said, bouncing excitedly in her chair. "Can he, Mommy? Can Davian watch the sunset with us?"

Between Davian's startled look and Adella's sly grin, Cate couldn't help laughing. "Fine. It's a free ship. Watch if you want."

Not exactly a romantic invitation, but Cate hadn't intended it to be.

They continued eating, Adella chattering away about what she and Davian had seen before Cate's arrival. Every so often Cate hazarded a glance up to find Davian watching their daughter, a look of pure captivation on his face. It would've been amazing if the rest of their situation hadn't been such a mess.

Finally, Adella finished her meal and asked if she could go play with the rest of her toys near the wall of the boat. Cate let her, keeping an eye on her daughter from the table. She and Davian sat across from each other now as the sun crept lower toward the horizon.

"Cate?"

His voice interrupted her thoughts and she looked over to find him watching her expectantly. Crap. Once again, she'd let herself get distracted and missed what someone was saying. So frustrating. This wasn't her, dammit. But the second her eyes met Davian's she wished they hadn't because suddenly he was too close and yes, too hot, for her to handle.

"You've got some butter on your face," he said, holding out a napkin.

"Oh." She took the napkin and wiped her mouth where he'd indicated. "Gone?"

"No."

She tried again. "How about now?"

He squinted over at her. "Still there. Let me try."

Davian snatched the napkin back from her before she could stop him, then stood to lean over the table toward her, lifting her chin gently with one hand while he brushed the napkin lightly over the corner of her mouth with the other. Her eyelids fluttered closed against her will as intoxicating sensation flooded her system. It had been so long, too long since someone had touched her the way Davian did. With such care and kindness and…

Time slowed as their gazes locked and the air between them sizzled. His eyes flicked to her mouth then back again, and Cate swallowed hard, fresh warmth tingling through her midsection. The same desire swarming inside her filled Davian's blue eyes as well, heating them. His gaze seemed to go darker then, still locked on Cate's face, his entire expression changing from intense concern to intense need. Davian leaned in a few inches more, so close that Cate could feel his breath on her cheeks. The napkin fell to the table, only to be replaced by Davian's hand cupping her cheek. They shouldn't be doing this. It was craziness. And Adella was right there, playing with her toys and ignoring them completely, but still.

This wasn't good. Not because she didn't want Davian too. In truth, she'd never really stopped wanting him, even after five years. But because right then, she wanted him too much. Anything that might happen between them on this charter couldn't last. He was going back to his country and his hospital, and she was going back to Boston to start her clinic. They'd keep in touch for Adella, but that was about it. This was just a remembrance of old feelings, an old life, making them imagine things that weren't there. There was no future in this. None. Not beyond a short-lived explosion of heat flaring hot and heavy between them, that would soon fizzle to nothing when they went their separate ways. Same as before.

But no matter how many times her logical mind shouted those things, Cate couldn't seem to make herself move away. He stayed where he was, watching, waiting, until finally, Davian leaned all the way in and kissed her, sending her blood racing and her heart pounding and man, oh, man… It was good.

Sweet and soft and so very sexy.

At least until…

"Mommy! Look at the sunset!" Adella yelled, running up to tug on the leg of Cate's shorts. "There's so many different colors."

A bit flummoxed by passion, Cate blinked at Davian for a few seconds before backing off and picking up her daughter, doing her best to concentrate on the moment, and not the man still standing behind her, looking as discombobulated as Cate felt.

Wow. That kiss had been everything she'd remember with Davian and more.

Which meant she couldn't let it happen again.

CHAPTER SEVEN

THEY WERE AT sea the next day. Not because they had a long voyage to reach their next destination, but because some of the members of the King's entourage wanted to play with the water toys. Jet Skis, a Jetlev, water skis, wakeboards, floats, hydrofoils, paddleboards, Seabobs, even a huge inflatable slide hung from the uppermost deck of the yacht down to the water—it had all been put out by the deck crew for their guests' entertainment. The sun was out, the water was relatively warm and it looked to be a great day of sun and fun.

For everyone except Davian, that was. He was still too focused on the almost-kiss last night with Cate to think of anything other than her and the fact that even after all these years his feelings for her were still just as strong. Even now, when he closed his eyes, he swore he could feel her breath on his face, see the tiny shudder that ran through her when his fingertips traced her cheek, the catch of her breath when he'd leaned in close, closer, so close that his lips nearly met hers and…

"Look out below!" Maybrook, one of his father's friends and an earl, yelled before barreling down the water slide and splashing into the water. Raucous laughter followed from the others already in the sea below. They'd all been drinking for a while now, even though it was just barely noon.

Davian sighed and shook his head before returning his attention to the article he'd been reading. Of course, he could have been staring at a page full of cartoons for all his heart was in it right then. Normally, he loved reading all the technical aspects of new procedures, committing them to memory for later trial. But each time his thoughts started to drift, it was not to the OR where he performed his procedures, but to Cate.

Always Cate.

Or more precisely, at that point, why she continually changed the subject or refused to delve deeper into the issues surrounding their daughter, Adella.

Their daughter.

My daughter.

It still shocked him to say those words, despite repeating them in his head over and over and knowing in his heart it was true. Adella was his. She could have been his twin at that age. No denying it. But accepting it and feeling one hundred percent comfortable with the idea were two different things. Davian loved children. Always had. He'd just not expected to find out he had one out of the blue like this. And the fact that Cate still seemed wary of him didn't help matters. Yes, he'd hurt her. Yes, he was sorry for it. Sorrier than she could ever know. But if they were going to make this work, somehow, they had to get past that and move forward.

And speaking of moving forward…

"Let's try this again," Maybrook said, slurring his words slightly as he walked over to the inflatable slide once more. Puddles formed around his wet footprints on the wooden deck and his steps swayed a bit as he approached the area where two deckhands were positioned to help the guests up the steps to the top of the slide. "Can't let Shorington show me up, eh, Davie?"

Davian raised one hand in brief acknowledgment but didn't look up from his journal. He hated the nickname Davie and had told Maybrook on several occasions, to no avail. Still, the man was one of his father's oldest and dearest friends so there wasn't much he could do about it now.

"Gonna climb back up here like this…" Maybrook said from behind Davian.

"Sir, please wait a moment while we straighten the slide. The last wind gust— Sir!" one of the deckhands shouted.

The next thing Davian heard was a loud thud and a woman's scream. He was up and out of his chair in a second, his journal tossed aside without another thought in the face of a possible emergency. "What's wrong?" he said, hurrying over to where the two ashen-faced deckhands were staring down at the deck below theirs. "What's happened?"

"We told him to wait, sir," the one deckhand said. "The wind gust had twisted the slide and we were trying to straighten it, but he climbed up anyway and…"

One glance over the railing at the still body of Lord Maybrook on the deck below had adrenaline flooding Davian's system. He switched into surgeon mode immediately. "Call emergency. We need a medevac here ASAP."

Then he was jogging down the stairs to the lower deck, heart pounding in his ears in time with his steps. It had to be at least a fifteen-foot fall from the uppermost sundeck where they'd been down to here. And the teakwood decking was hard. Not good. Not good at all. He ran over to where the man lay prone, his chest barely rising and falling.

"Maybrook," Davian said, palpating his head

and neck, searching for injuries. "Maybrook, can you hear me?"

"What's happened?" Cate asked, running over to kneel on the other side of the patient.

Davian filled her in on the slide incident then took her stethoscope to listen to the man's lungs. "Shallow respirations. So far, he's remained unconscious and unresponsive."

"Sir! Sir!" Cate patted the man's cheeks again. "Sir, this is Dr. Neves. Can you answer me?"

Maybrook moaned a little then began flailing his arms and legs, nearly knocking Cate over. Davian moved fast to pin them down so Maybrook wouldn't hurt himself or them. The man's eyes flickered open, dazed and confused.

"Maybrook," Davian said, staring down into the older man's face. "It's Davian. You've had a fall and you're hurt. We're trying to help you. Please stay still."

"Medevac is on the way," one of the deckhands said, keeping the other guests off to the side, including Maybrook's sobbing wife. "Should be here in five minutes."

"Sir, can you tell me where it hurts?" Cate asked opening the man's life vest to palpate his chest. "Here? Or what about here?"

"Yes! There! Dammit, that hurts. Ouch!" Maybrook yelled, the scent of alcohol heavy on his breath. They could talk to the crew later about the hazards of letting guests under the influence use the water toys, not that Maybrook would have listened. But right now everything had to be about saving their patient's life.

"Abdomen tender," Cate noted. "Also swollen. I'm guessing we've got some internal bleeding going on in there too."

"Do you have a catheter in that medical pack?" Davian asked, hiking his chin toward the black bag near Cate's feet.

"I do."

"Okay." Davian glanced over to where a small crowd had gathered on the deck. "Can you please move everyone away? We need to perform a procedure on the patient to assess his internal injuries."

The deckhands quickly herded the others away from the scene, Maybrook's wife still crying softly into Davian's mother's shoulder.

"We need to get a catheter in him and see if there's blood in his urine," Davian said, moving to the medical kit for the necessary supplies. Once he'd gloved up and gotten the equipment, he moved back to Maybrook and inserted the catheter. It was no sooner in than bright red blood filled the tube. "We have blood. I'm guessing a liver laceration and probably kidney injury as well."

"Dammit. Okay." Cate continued her steady, thorough exam of the man's torso. "Sir, where else does it hurt?"

"My back!" Maybrook said. "My back is killing me. Can I turn onto my side?"

"No." Davian positioned himself over the man's torso to prevent him from moving again. "Maybrook, listen to me. You've had a fall. A pretty bad one. You can't move until the medics get here or you could risk hurting yourself even more. Just lay still, all right?"

Cate finished her assessment then sat back, catching Davian's eye. They both had their game faces on because of the emergency. Even during the most difficult cases, the physician had to keep control, otherwise the patient's chances of making it were almost nil. But he could see in her eyes the seriousness of Maybrook's condition. They'd already confirmed internal bleeding, which meant they had perhaps a fifteen- to twenty-minute window to get him to a medical facility and into surgery or he could bleed out and die.

Cate took the stethoscope back from Davian and checked Maybrook's blood pressure. "It's low. Eighty over sixty. From the internal bleeding most likely."

"I need to get up," Maybrook said, struggling

against Davian. "I don't want my wife to see me like this. I have an image to protect."

Davian opened his mouth to tell the man that when your life was falling apart, image meant nothing. He should know. But before he could, the whomp-whomp-whomp of the approaching medevac helicopter stopped him. Soon, the chopper landed on the aft deck helipad a short distance away and two medics raced up to where Cate and Davian were working on Maybrook. He filled them in on what he knew.

"Sixty-two-year-old male fell from a height of about fifteen feet and landed on his back. Exam shows suspected internal bleeding, possibly liver and kidney, and there is blood in his urine. He complains of back pain also. Loss of consciousness and some combativeness and disorientation."

"What's happening with my husband?" Maybrook's wife cried out, a brightly colored beach towel wrapped around her still-wet, bathing suit–clad body. She had on flip-flops and a sun hat, about as far away from courtly glitz and glamour as a person could be. In the end, they were all just people, doing the best they could to get by, Davian realized. Same as him. He moved aside as the medics got Maybrook carefully loaded onto a body board and started an

IV in his arm then trundled him off to the waiting chopper.

"Wait!" Maybrook's wife called. "I want to go with him."

The medics hurried her aboard the helicopter alongside her husband then quickly took off for the shore and an awaiting surgical team at the hospital there who'd been briefed on the situation.

Afterward, Davian and Cate stood with the others, watching the chopper recede into the distance, the air oddly silent except for the caw of seagulls and the whistle of the wind.

Davian didn't realize until someone bumped his arm that his father was standing beside him, looking gruff and visibly shaken. He turned and guided his father to a nearby chair to sit in. "You should rest. That was quite a nasty ordeal."

"Will he be all right?" the King asked, seemingly having aged ten years in the past ten minutes.

"I don't know," Davian said, honestly, crouching beside his father. "But he's in good hands with the surgeons. I'll call later and get an update on him."

His father nodded gravely. "Thank God you were here, son."

"It's my job," Davian said.

"It's your calling," his father said. And for the

first time, Davian felt seen. Medicine was his calling. Always had been, but he'd never imagined his father recognizing that and acknowledging it. Then as quickly as the moment had arrived, it disappeared, and his father visibly withdrew again behind his walls of kingly distance. The King cleared his throat and stood, gripping the chair back. "Make sure this never leaks into the press."

Davian rocked back on his heels and hung his head. There it was again. The press. Always the press. His father's good friend had been badly injured and still, all his father was worried about was if the story would be leaked. Enough. This was exactly why Davian wanted no more of the royal life. Putting image above all else. And it nudged him one step closer to renouncing it all for good.

"Well, that was not how I pictured my lunch hour going," Cate said as she cleaned up the medical supplies strewn on the deck from the emergency. "How about you?"

Davian had withdrawn again, closing himself off behind those walls of his, after talking to his father. Her heart ached for him a little that they didn't get along, but then at least he had his father there. It was more than she'd had growing up.

"Hmm." He walked back over to help her. "You did good work there, Doctor."

"As did you." She smiled. If she was being truthful, she'd always loved working with Davian because they made each other better. They had a healthy competition that kept them both performing at the top of their games. "Good call with the catheter."

"Thanks."

"Is your father okay?" she asked as she zipped up an outside pocket on the med pack.

"He'll be fine." Davian frowned then straightened, holding out a hand to help Cate up. "Got to project that strong image, you know."

There was a brittleness to his tone that pricked her heart. "Must be exhausting, always being strong like that."

"It is," he said, following her back down to the clinic belowdecks.

Having him there, in her space was…odd. Obviously, with the whole Adella issue out there now, they'd be spending more time together this charter, but still. Cate had been on her own a long time and having Davian there now felt strange. Not bad necessarily, but different. Plus, she was still having a hard time dealing with all the ramifications of telling him about his daughter. It was too late now, but perhaps she shouldn't have told him. Or should have chosen her moment better. But then, when would exactly the right time be to tell a man that he had a five-year-old daughter he never knew about?

Ugh. Those thoughts had kept Cate tossing and turning all last night and still had her tied in knots today. She unlocked the clinic door and pushed inside, flipping the lights on and setting the med pack down on the floor near the supply closet for refilling, as Davian followed her inside then closed the door behind them. Dr. Bryant had the day off and Carrie was on break so that left just Cate to man the clinic at present. Probably a good thing, since her heart was racing, and it had nothing to do with the trek down here and everything to do with the man across from her who seemed to suck up all the oxygen in the room.

"It makes you think, doesn't it?" Davian said, sinking down into one of the chairs near the door in their makeshift waiting room. "An accident like that."

"How do you mean?" she asked, pulling a couple bottles of water out of a small fridge behind the reception desk. Cate handed one to Davian then took a seat in the chair beside his.

"Just how things can change so quickly, out of the blue."

She nodded and sipped her water. "That's certainly true in our case."

"Yes, it is."

They sat in silence a moment, Davian leaning forward to rest his forearms atop his thighs, his hands between his knees. He took a deep breath then looked back at her over his shoulder. "How are you coping with it all?"

"Us, you mean?" She shrugged. "Okay, I guess. It's a lot. How about you?"

He bit his lower lip then sat back, his arm brushing hers as he did so, sending shocks of unwanted awareness through her body. Coping with the mental reality of having Davian back in her life was enough at present. She didn't need the physical and emotional realities jamming up her circuits too. Except, her body seemed to have other ideas. Davian ran a hand through his dark hair then stared up at the ceiling. "I don't know, Cate. I really don't. I'd like to say that I'm overjoyed by the news of Adella, but that would be a lie."

Cate's posture stiffened. "You said you were happy."

"I am happy. I'm also just...confused. Torn." He shook his head and closed his eyes. "I'm trying to stay present here for this. To keep you in the loop with what I'm feeling and thinking. Figure that's the least I can do after shutting you out all those years ago. But it's hard."

"I know." She fiddled with the label on her bottle, picking at one corner.

"You do?"

He was looking at her now. Even though she was staring at her bottle she could feel his gaze, burning into her temple.

She sighed and looked over at him. It would be so easy, to let him in again, to talk to him. Davian had always been such a good listener, despite how things had ended with them. But no. She couldn't trust him again, certainly not so quickly. Still, he was watching her with such concern in his eyes that she felt like she should give him something, so she said, "I do. I mean, growing up an only child of a single mom, you learn to keep things in."

Not a lie. Not the complete truth either.

He blinked at her a few times, then nodded. "I can see that. I remember you talking about her back in residency. How is your mom?"

"Good. Still living in Boston. She keeps an eye on my house for me while we're away."

"That's convenient."

"Yep."

Another awkward silence ensued, all the things that hadn't been said hanging heavy between them like an overfilled clothesline. Finally,

Davian blurted out, "I'm going to talk to my parents before this trip is over and tell them that I'm leaving royal life."

Cate looked over at him, her brows knit. "What? Why?"

"Because it's the right decision for me. I've felt it for quite some time, but now with Adella, I know it's what I must do. I don't want to expose her to all the horrible things that happened to me growing up in that life." He sighed and shook his head. "The deception, the unfair duty, the false bravado. I just want to practice medicine and have a normal life. And I want Adella to have a normal life too."

Her alarm bells went off before she could stop them. Hearing Davian talk so passionately about a future with their daughter brought out her mama bear side again and Cate pushed to her feet, her tone cool. "Well, just remember that I'm the one who sets the ground rules here. I decide what does and does not happen in Adella's future, whether you remain a prince or not. And I'll still be the one deciding when we tell her about you. Understood?"

Davian narrowed his gaze on her and for a moment, Cate worried she'd pushed too far. But then he sighed and stood as well, his small smile conciliatory. "Yes, Cate. I understand. But you should also know that I plan to be so charming and indispensable that you and Adella won't be able to live without me."

Cate watched as he opened the door and walked out, still staring after him as he retreated down the hallway.

Unfortunately, not being able to live without him was exactly what she feared most.

CHAPTER EIGHT

THE NEXT MORNING, bright and early, Davian was up and ready to go ashore. But first he needed to see his parents off with their security team. Unfortunately, though, when he arrived on deck for breakfast, Noah was waiting for him. He'd gotten word from the hospital onshore that Lord Maybrook had come through surgery well and his condition had improved, which was an encouraging sign.

"Where are the King and Queen?" Davian asked, frowning.

"Still abed. Your father says he's not up to traipsing around Monaco today and wishes to stay on board the ship instead. Your mother agrees. After everything that happened yesterday, they don't feel up to leaving."

"Are you sure?" Concern edged Davian's tone. When he'd talked to his father the night before, they'd still been excited to go into Monte Carlo and Davian had worked hard to arrange everything they wanted to do, including having lunch with old friends they'd not seen in years at a private villa. "Is everything all right? My father is feeling all right?"

"The King said yes, Your Highness," Noah said. "Just that they wished to stay on the ship instead. They said not to change your plans at all, and they would see you at dinner tonight."

And now Davian's concern deepened to worry. His father loved to travel and his mother loved to shop. Both were possible today, so them deciding not to go was a huge red flag. Between his father's health issues and the assassination threats, stress levels were through the roof for his family. Questioning the chief steward about it though wouldn't get him any further, so Davian decided to go straight to the source.

"Thank you, Noah. If Dr. Neves and her daughter arrive, please tell them to wait. I'll be right back."

"Yes, Your Highness."

Davian hurried downstairs to the master suite and knocked on the door. "Mother, Father? It's Davian. May I come in?"

The door opened slightly a moment later to his mother, still in her silk dressing gown, looking up at him through the crack. "Yes, dear. What is it?"

"I was told you won't be going ashore today. Is everything all right?"

"Yes, dear," his mother said, not moving to allow the door to open wider. "We're fine. Just want to stay here and relax a bit. Enjoy the sunshine."

On the surface, it sounded plausible enough, but Davian was still wary. "What about your friends? They were so excited to see you both today and went to a lot of trouble to get the villa ready for your visit."

"I've called them already to explain. They're going to come to the yacht for lunch instead, dear. All taken care of."

"Oh." Davian didn't have a response for that. He tried to lean around his mother to see his father in the room but couldn't. "What about Father? Is he feeling well?"

"Fine, son," came a deep voice echoing out of the suite. "Just catching up on some business emails while I'm resting," his father said. "Let the boy in, Arabella. You know how he worries."

His mother moved aside then and opened the door so Davian could see his father stretched out atop the huge king-size bed. Pillows were stacked up behind him, propping him up so he could work on his tablet comfortably. He too had a silk dressing gown on over black silk pants and glasses so he could see the screen better

He appeared healthy and hearty, despite Davian's concerns.

Okay. Maybe he was projecting some of his own nerves about the day ahead with Cate and Adella onto a situation where they weren't warranted. Being a doctor was sometimes a double-edged sword. You sometimes saw emergencies where there were none, especially with those closest to you. It seemed that was what was happening here.

Davian took a deep breath then raked a hand through his hair. "Okay. Sorry. Sounds like you two have things all squared away then. But please call me if you need anything, yes? I'll have my phone with me all day."

"Thank you, dear," his mother said, looking him up and down with a smile. He'd dressed casually today in a loose-fitting Hawaiian-style shirt and cargo shorts, sandals on his feet. "Good to see you having some fun for a change. Enjoy yourself."

"Thanks. I hope to," Davian said, turning to leave.

"Son, come here." His father's voice stopped him. "I have some questions."

He exhaled slowly then walked into the master cabin to stand by the side of the bed. "Yes, Father?"

"This woman you're going with, Dr. Neves. You knew her in college?" his father asked.

"Yes. We did our residency together at Stanford." *Or most of it, anyway, until you called me home abruptly.* Davian left that last part out. "She's a friend. Why?"

"Just be careful, son," his father said, looking up at Davian over the rim of his glasses. "The last thing we need right now is a scandal."

It took most of his effort to bite back his response to that. The only scandals Davian had ever been involved in at the palace had been ones of his father's PR team's invention. Anger burned in his gut before he extinguished it. The cruise would be over in a few days, then they could get back to their normal lives again and Davian could keep more distance between himself and his royal duty. Until then, it was best to just grin and bear it. "Today will be scandal free, I promise. She'll have her five-year-old daughter there. Hard to be scandalous with kids around."

"Hmm," his father said, sounding thoroughly unconvinced, which rubbed Davian wrong, but nothing to do for it except leave. "Bring her to dinner tonight. I want to meet her myself."

"Uh, okay. I'll do that," Davian said, kissing his mother briefly on the cheek before heading upstairs again to find Cate and Adella waiting for him near the passerelle. They were wearing matching white tops and jean shorts, with white sneakers. Davian had a hard time looking away from Cate's long, bare legs, but forced himself to, smiling as he approached. "Good morning, ladies. Are we ready for an adventure?"

"Yes, please," Adella said, letting go of Cate's hand to clap. "I want an adventure, Davian!"

"Then you shall have one, Princess!" He laughed and swooped her up in his arms as she giggled and held on to him tight. His chest squeezed at the sweetness of holding his daughter for the first time. Then he glanced at Cate and saw the flicker of wariness in her green eyes and vowed to do whatever he must to make that disappear by the end of the day. His gaze dropped to her pink lips for a second, remembering their kiss from the night before—hot, electric and far too brief—then he shoved that aside too. If things went to plan, there'd be no time for kissing today. Besides, with Adella there and the fact that there were still so many unknowns between him and Cate, no kissing was probably a good idea, regardless of how his heart raced at the thought. She smiled and gestured toward the passerelle extending to the concrete dock on the other side. "Shall we go?"

The principality of Monaco was not big, but what it lacked in size, it made up for in style. One of the most affluent spots in the world, with its palace and grand casino, it was also rich in nature. Today, Davian had designed a private tour for them to see it all.

They started at the Palais du Prince, the residence of the royal family of Monaco. While Davian had grown up in his own family's smaller and more rugged castle back in Ruclecia, this palace was much older and much more ornate than any in his homeland. Built in the thirteenth century as a Genoese fortress, the Palais du Prince overlooked the whole of Monaco from its lofty perch, allowing for great views of the city of Monte Carlo and the sea below. As they walked through the gilded halls and the lush Blue Room, Cate whispered and pointed out things to Adella, who seemed enthralled with it all. But it wasn't until they reached the throne room, with its huge gold and red velvet throne at the front, that Adella said, "Is that where you sit, Davian?"

Eyes wide, he looked over at Cate, who seemed as shocked as he was that Adella knew his status. He crouched beside her and said, "No, I don't sit on a throne like that, Princess. My father does. And how did you know that?"

"Noah told me about you," Adella said, sounding very forthright. "He said you're nobility."

"Ah." Davian straightened. "Right," he said, leading them out of the throne room toward the exit. "Where should we go next? How about the aquarium?"

"Is that where they have all the fish?" Adella asked, taking hold of Davian's hand, so she was between both him and Cate. "I want to see a shark. Do they have a shark, Mommy?"

"I don't know, sweetie. I guess we'll find out."

Not only did they have sharks, but they also had a huge cylindrical tank filled with jellyfish, an extensive coral exhibit, a rehab center for injured sea turtles, and a gorgeous observation deck with incredible views of the Mediterranean. There were also numerous exhibits about the north and south poles and climate change, something Davian and his older brother were passionate about as well. It was all very well done and informative and gave Davian lots of ideas to talk to his brother about when he got back to Ruclecia—things they could do similarly in their own country to bring in more tourists while also helping the planet. By the time they were done there and heading to lunch, they were all starving.

"Mommy!" Adella said in the private chauffeured van Davian had rented for their use for the day. "Did you see me walking on those whale skeletons? That was so cool!"

"I did, sweetie." Cate laughed and kissed the

top of Adella's head. "It's amazing what they can do with those lights now."

"Isn't it?" Davian said, his arm draped along the back of the seat, his fingers grazing Cate's shoulder as Adella sat between them. It felt so natural and normal and right, them being together like this. Almost like a real family. He hadn't realized how much he craved that until now. "Have you seen the Van Gogh immersive exhibition that uses the same technology?"

"Yes. My mom and I went when it came to Boston and it was incredible. Adella was still too young to remember it, but she was there too."

"Where was I, Mommy?" Adella asked, frowning as she looked up from playing with her stuffed toys. In addition to her monkey, now she also had a stuffed octopus that Davian had bought for her at the aquarium. "And who's Van Gogh?"

"He's a famous artist, sweetie," Cate said, stroking Adella's hair back from her face. It was pulled back into a ponytail, but some strands had come loose. "And you were with Grandmom and me at the exhibit of his work when you were just a baby."

"Oh. I don't remember that." Adella fiddled with her toys again before adding, "Davian should come with us next time too. You'll come too, won't you, Davian?"

"I… Uh…" He looked from Adella to Cate then back again. "We'll see, Princess."

The little girl sighed. "I don't have a daddy, you know."

Talk about a sucker punch to the gut. All the air huffed out of Davian's lungs as he struggled with how to handle that. Part of him wanted to scoop his daughter up and say, *Yes, you do have a father. Me. Right here. And I'll never leave you again.* But the other part of him, the part trained for years to look out for the family first, held him back. Once that secret was out of the box, it couldn't be put back in again. For the moment, only he and Cate knew, and Davian wanted to keep it that way until they'd worked out all the details of handling it going forward. Only then did he plan to tell Adella, followed by his parents and brother, then finally the rest of the world.

So, instead of answering her question, Davian changed subjects by asking one of his own. "Okay. Who's hungry?"

The relief on Cate's face mirrored his own when Adella quickly raised her hand, her former melancholy apparently forgotten. "Me! I'm so hungry!"

"Great." Davian leaned closer to the driver to whisper something to him then sat back again. "We should be there shortly."

A few minutes later, they pulled up in front

of a long, narrow alleyway packed on both sides with shops and vendors. They got out and walked through the crowds, stopping every so often to look at items on sale or to window-shop. Finally, they went around a slight bend and the smells of garlic and fresh baked bread made Davian's stomach rumble.

"Oh, that smells good!" Cate said, inhaling deep. "Where are we going?"

"Just to the best pizza place in all of Monaco!" He took Adella's hand and they walked the little girl between them up to a doorway with a white awning over the top reading La Tavernetta. The hostess inside recognized Davian from his last trip there a few years earlier with this brother and rushed over to give him a hug. They were an old Italian family who'd run the little restaurant for years. Not many tourists knew about it, but all the locals did, which meant the food was excellent. They were shown to a quiet table in the corner, near the windows, where they could people watch while they ate. They ordered drinks and pizza, then chatted while they waited for their food.

"How did you know about this place?" Cate asked between sips of her water.

"This is one of my favorite places in Monaco," Davian said, smiling. "My brother and I discovered it while visiting here with our parents years ago and I've kept coming back since. It's a good spot to just sit and wonder about things." He sighed. "And when my life fell apart during residency, I'd come here alone for privacy. It was my sanctuary."

"It's good that you had a place of your own to go to," Cate said. "And that you had your brother to hang out with. Are you two still close?"

"Not as much as we were back then," Davian said, his chest squeezing a bit with nostalgia. "When we were kids, it was like us against the world. But as we grew older, he was put on track to become King and I was left more to my own devices." He snorted. "Well, at least until they needed me to quell an emergency in the PR department."

Cate reached over and took his hand, frowning. "And your brother was okay with that? Them using you, I mean?"

"No. Of course not." He took a deep breath and put his head back, closing his eyes. "But as Crown Prince, Arthur had about as much power to stop the royal press machine as I did back then. He tried to be as supportive as possible, telling me that we'd fix whatever had broken once the crisis was over, but then he'd be taken away to do a diplomacy visit or give a speech or visit some dignitary and I'd still have a mess on my hands." Her fingers tightened around his gently in a show of support. "Anyway, I'm sure that's part of the reason why I acted out in my teens, partied so much. Just to forget it all for a while."

"I'm so sorry, Davian. I had no idea you went through all that. You deserved better."

His breath caught at the tender conviction in her tone, and he wanted nothing more than to pull her into his arms and hold her close but didn't dare. Not yet.

Her gaze flicked from his to scan the interior, the plain white walls, the curved ceiling, the simple, local paintings hanging around the space, and she smiled. She looked even more beautiful today, if that were possible, relaxed and enjoying herself—at least until his little confession—and Davian's heart squeezed. He wanted to get the spotlight off himself and learn more about her. To know everything there was to know about Cate Neves. "It must be hard, traveling so much with charters. Do you miss your mother?"

"Sometimes." Cate looked at him, blinking for a second like it took her that moment to register what he'd said. Then her cheeks flushed pink, and her gaze darted away again. "I talk to her at least once a week on the phone, so that helps."

Davian wished she'd let him in, reveal more about herself, but he didn't want to push. As much as he was press-phobic, he knew trust was an issue for her and stressing her out about it would only make it worse. She'd tell him more when she was ready.

"And here we are," their server said, setting a tray full of food on a stand nearby. The man set out plates and silverware, then a large stone-fired margherita pizza and a fresh salad.

Hungry, they all dug into their food, not taking much time to converse until out of the blue Adella said, "Where do the baby whales we saw in the aquarium come from?"

He nearly choked on a bite of pizza, coughing into his napkin then taking a big swig of soda to cover it. "Uh…"

"Finish your food, sweetie," Cate intervened, giving Davian a little wink. "We can have crème brûlée for dessert."

"Creamy what?" Adella scrunched her nose.

"Crème brûlée," Cate repeated, her soft pink lips forming all sorts of interesting shapes that had Davian looking away fast to avoid embarrassing himself again. "It's like vanilla custard, but with a crunchy layer of toasted sugar on top."

"Oh, yes! I want to try that, Mommy!"

To prove it, Adella shoved a large bite of pizza into her mouth and chewed fast, making both Cate and Davian laugh. "A girl after my own heart," he said, reaching over to ruffle Adella's hair. There was a slight curl to it, just like his. One more way they were alike.

After they finished lunch, Davian paid the bill, then they went back out to the rental van again to head to their afternoon destination, Les Jardins Saint Martin. The lovely gardens were located right next to the aquarium, but Davian had thought it might be too much to do all at once with little Adella, and he'd been right. Before they even reached their last destination, Adella fell asleep in the van, her toys clutched to her chest to keep them safe. When they got to the gardens, which stretched along the coastline near Le Rocher and featured stunning views of the Mediterranean, Davian hired a stroller to carry Adella in to save his and Cate's arms. Their daughter didn't even wake up when they transferred her, showing how tired out she was.

Strolling the quiet, peaceful paths was the perfect ending to a lovely day. Sun-dappled trails hugging the Rock of Monaco led them through the gardens themselves, past statues, fountains, Aleppo pines, yellow agave and even the famed Monaco Cathedral. Cate had had her phone out all day, snapping pictures for posterity. Normally, Davian shied away from cameras, but he trusted Cate and knew they were for her own memories, nothing more.

They stopped to gaze out over the sea near the statue of Prince Albert as a sailor near the center of the gardens and took a seat on a bench to rest a while before heading back to the van.

Cate stared out to sea, the breeze gently ruffling her hair, and if circumstances had been different, Davian would've pulled her into his side and inhaled her scent. Soap and lemons. As it was, they sat side by side with silence stretching between them like a sail.

Finally, she said, "Thank you, Davian. For bringing us here today. It was wonderful."

"I'm glad you liked it." He exhaled slowly, his shoulders slumping as he thought about returning to the yacht. "I'm worried about my father."

She looked over at him, frowning behind her sunglasses. "Why? What happened?"

"They didn't go on their tour today. The one I spent days planning for them. I don't care about the tour, but it's not like them to cancel plans with friends." He shook his head and looked out over the blue waters that stretched to the horizon, sunlight sparkling atop them. "I told you about his heart attack and bypass and I'm concerned he's having problems again."

"Did you ask him about it?"

"Yes. This morning before we left. Both he and my mother said he was fine, but..."

"You don't believe them?"

"No, I don't." Davian looked away. "It wouldn't

be the first time they kept me out of the loop on things."

"No, I guess it wouldn't." Cate watched him a moment, then said, "I'm sorry about how they treated you in residency. That wasn't right."

"No, it wasn't." He took a deep breath then reached for her hand on the bench, glad when she didn't pull away. "And I'm sorry for everything I've put you through, Cate. None of this was ever my intention. I hope you know that now."

She gave a small nod, staring down at their entwined fingers on the white stone bench. "I never told you back in residency, but after my father walked out on us, I still remember seeing him with his new family sometimes, so happy and carefree, so different from how he was with us." She gave a mirthless laugh. "You know, he never once told me he was sorry. Sorry about walking away, sorry about lying to us. Just good-bye and that was that. He threw us away like we were trash, Davian. Like we didn't matter at all. I never want Adella to go through feeling that way. That's why I'm so careful with her." She took a deep breath then released it. "That's why I have such a hard time trusting people."

He didn't respond, just stroked his thumb over her wrist and squeezed her fingers, letting her know he was there to support her, if needed.

"I've done well raising Adella on my own, so

it's not easy for me to let someone into our lives now. Especially you...after what happened." She inhaled and looked up at him, his face reflected in her sunglass lenses. "But after talking with you, hearing your side of things..."

"Davian?" Adella's little voice, still groggy with sleep, said from the stroller. "Can we go look at those flowers? The pretty pink ones by the wall?" She squirmed in her seat, the restraints keeping her from getting out by herself. "Pink's my favorite color."

He swallowed hard and looked to Cate for guidance or permission or both. She gave a subtle nod and Davian smiled. He wasn't sure how they'd navigate this new path going forward, but he did want to try. With every bone in his body. "Sure, Princess. Let me just get you out of this stroller and we'll go look at them."

Cate stayed back on the bench with the stroller watching her daughter and Davian whispering to each other about the flowers and Adella listening raptly to Davian as he explained to her about the bees and pollination. It would be obvious to anyone who saw the two together that they were related—same eyes, same coloring, same intense expression when they were consumed with a topic that interested them—but Cate couldn't bring herself to care about the risks that might cause. Not then. Not when joy bubbled in her bloodstream to see Adella so happy with her father.

Until that moment, the idea that her daughter might be missing out on important life lessons because she was without her father had been more of a nebulous thing, something to deal with down the road. But now it was plain as day. Davian had a way of relating to Adella that was different than Cate, but just as important. More as a teacher, a confidant, a friend. And while Cate hoped that her daughter saw her as all those things too, it was unique with Davian.

Even more impressive to her was the fact of how available Davian made himself to Adella. Never balking at her constant questions, never hesitating to do whatever Adella asked of him, no matter how silly. The fact that a prince of Ruclecia was currently sitting on the ground talking to a bumblebee for his daughter's amusement was proof enough of that. He was there. Present. In ways Cate's own father had never been for her. And perhaps it was that fact, more than anything else, that finally made something click inside her. Finally pushed her suspicions and skepticism aside and made Cate realize that telling Adella that Davian was her father was the right thing to do.

She inhaled deep, expecting the same rush of

tension that usually accompanied that thought to course through her, but it never came. Huh. Cate exhaled through her nose, still watching Adella and Davian move on to a different set of flowers, these white and yellow and purple. Davian seemed to know the names of all of them and shared little tidbits of information about the plants with Adella, delighting her and keeping her in a state of amazed curiosity. No small feat with a five-year-old.

No. Telling their daughter the truth was the right thing to do. After all, Cate had shared more with Davian today about her own father and the pain that seeing him with a new family, a different family, had caused her. As if Cate and her mother were a mistake and his new family was a do-over. But she'd wanted him to know, wanted Davian to have all the facts about her and her past before he made a decision about his future with Adella. Because for Cate, there was no in between. Davian had to be all in or all out. No hesitation. No second-guessing afterward. She'd been through that searing, scalding shame, that feeling of utter, gut-wrenching abandonment, and she would never, ever put her precious Adella through that.

When Adella and Davian returned to her at last and they got their daughter secured back in the stroller, they started back down toward the yacht. More people had arrived, it seemed, and the footpaths were more crowded, forcing her and Davian to walk closer together, their shoulders brushing with each step. Adella was chattering away to herself about the flowers and the bees and a comfortable silence settled between them.

At least until Cate said the words she needed to say. "Davian, I've been thinking."

He chuckled and smiled over at her. "Uh-oh."

"I'm serious." She gave him a playful swat on the arm then lowered her voice to make sure Adella wouldn't hear. "I have no idea how this will work, with us half a world apart, but Adella likes you and I think she should have a father in her life. You two are good together. I think we should tell her. About you being her father. If that's what you want too."

Davian's eyes widened and he stopped in the middle of the footpath, to the discontent of the people behind them. They moved over to the side, near a small flowering bush out of the flow of traffic and into a small private alcove in the shade. He looked astonished. A tad apprehensive too. But also excited. "Yes," he said. "I'd like that too."

"Good."

"Good."

They were closer here, closer than Cate had

realized initially. And with all the extra people around now, they had to wait a moment for a break in traffic to ease back onto the footpath. Still, Cate didn't mind. Neither did Davian apparently, since his gaze was still locked on hers, bluer than any sea she'd ever imagined. Time seemed to slow in their little paradise as he leaned in, his eyes flicking down to her lips, which were tingling as if she'd been stung. Then his mouth was on hers, soft and slow and lingering. Sweet and sinful and so very good all at the same time.

Davian pulled back a little. "Cate, I…"

Before he could finish she grabbed him by the front of his shirt and pulled him back to her to kiss him again, a bit harder this time.

When they parted this time, they were both breathless and grinning, their foreheads together.

Cate felt lighter than she had in days, years even, despite everything that had happened on this charter. Having Davian in her life again felt good, right. And she wasn't ready to give that up yet. "We should probably keep going," she said after a moment, smoothing his shirt back into place. "Wouldn't want you to be late for dinner."

"My parents want you to join us," he blurted out with less finesse than usual.

"What? Really?" Now it was Cate's turn to be astonished, her brows rising. "We've never dined with royalty. What if I pull a *Pretty Woman* and send a snail flying up against the wall?"

"I doubt that will happen." Davian leaned in to sneak one last, quick kiss then grinned. "From what I remember at Stanford, we attended several highbrow conferences together and you always had perfect table manners."

"Yeah, but this is with a king and queen."

"They're just my family, at the end of the day. Don't worry. My mom is great, and she can keep my dad reined in just fine."

"I hope so."

I hope so too.

"Mommy? Davian? Why are we stopped?" Adella asked, her tone starting to turn a tad whiny.

Yep. Definitely time to get back to the boat.

They left the alcove and returned to the footpath while Adella waved goodbye to all the flowers and bushes and bees on the way back to the park entrance. By the time the shuttle van arrived to take them to the dock, their daughter was snoozing. Davian took Cate's hand in his to help her into the van, then kept ahold of it, and Cate couldn't remember a time she'd felt more at peace.

CHAPTER NINE

CATE GAVE HERSELF a pep talk in the shower that night and as she got dressed, building her confidence for dining with a king and queen, but it all faltered when she entered the formal dining room on the main deck of the *Querencia*. Davian had told her eight sharp for dinner and she was right on time, but the rest of them were already there and seated at her arrival.

She was used to walking into exam rooms and boardrooms full of men and holding her head high and proving her point. But tonight felt more important than any procedure or treatment she'd ever performed in her life. And while she'd never been overly fixated on her appearance, she'd spent at least an hour going back and forth over what to wear and had ended up settling on the only thing that was appropriate for such an event, her standard little black dress. It wasn't anything spectacular, hitting just above her knees, with three-quarter-length sleeves and a boatneck that showed off her neck and collar-bones. But the fabric was good and so was the cut. She'd spent way too much money buying it at a fancy designer boutique in Boston before working on her first cruise ship at the insistence of her mother, who'd said she'd need something nice to wear to dinners at the captain's table. At the time, Cate had thought the suggestion silly, but now she was grateful for all those reruns of *The Love Boat* her mother had watched while Cate was growing up.

The whole day had felt like a magical dream. And in the gardens, it felt like things had changed between her and Davian, that they'd taken a major step forward. Not just in regard to telling Adella about her father, but also between Cate and Davian. They weren't lovers, but she felt closer to him now than she ever had before. Probably because for the first time, they saw each other. The real people, flaws and all. Not the polished, perfected facades they presented to the world. It left Cate feeling unsettled and unexpectedly energized to see what happened next. She wasn't a risk-taker by nature, but Davian seemed to bring out her boldness.

Stomach as tight as her smile, Cate dropped into a tiny curtsy at the top of the stairs and prayed for grace. "Good evening, Your Majesties."

Davian stood and grinned, warm and genuine, holding out a hand to her. "Ah, here's Dr. Neves now." When Cate drew nearer, he whispered in her ear, "You look lovely tonight."

Heat prickled her cheeks at the rush of warmth in her system, bringing back thoughts of their kisses earlier. She quickly pushed those away though as her gaze remained fixed on Davian's parents sitting directly across from them at the long table.

It was apparent that Davian had taken after his father in build and bone structure as King Phillipe stood, his attention zeroed in on Cate. "Dr. Neves. Nice to finally meet you," he said, his voice deeper and more accented than Davian's. He wore a plain black suit, white shirt, and dark tie emblazoned with tiny embroidered Ruclecian flags. "My son has told us so much about you."

Unsure how to greet royalty, Cate dipped into an awkward curtsy. "Thank you, Your Majesty. I'm honored to dine with you tonight."

"Oh, my dear," Davian's mother, Queen Arabella, said, her voice sweet and warm like honey. "No need to be so formal here. We're on vacation, after all." She stood as well and reached across the table to shake Cate's hand. She wore a pale blue sleeveless sheath dress that was deceptively simple but had to cost a lot of money, based on the perfect fit and how the color perfectly matched her eyes. The same shade as Davian's and Adella's. "You're as lovely as Davian said. Please do sit down."

Once they were all settled again and their drinks had been served, Cate hazarded a nervous smile at Davian beside her. "Adella couldn't stop talking about the trip today. She had a fabulous time, Davian. We both did. Thank you for showing us around Monaco."

"My pleasure."

Beneath the table, Davian reached over and took her hand, giving it a reassuring squeeze. Before today, Cate would've pulled away. But tonight, she could use all the support she could get, especially when King Phillipe began questioning her.

"Adella is your daughter, Dr. Neves?" he asked.

"Yes, Your Majesty," she replied. "And please, call me Cate."

Davian's father blinked at her, his expression unreadable. "And how old is your child?"

"She's five. A friend on the crew is watching her for me tonight."

"I see." The King sat back as the first course of their dinner was served, fine vegetable ravioli with amber consommé and spring herbs. He glanced over at his son and shook his head. "I may turn into a rabbit soon."

Davian chuckled. "Try it, Father. It's very

good. And vegetables are healthier for you." In a lower voice he said to Cate, "He's on a strict diet now because of his heart. He'll get used to it."

"It's delicious," Queen Arabella said, nodding to Noah, who stood near the wall to serve them as needed throughout the meal. "So fresh and well seasoned."

King Phillipe ate his two raviolis then sat back so Noah could clear his plate. "More meals like that and I'll waste away to nothing."

"I don't believe we need to worry," the Queen said loftily. "There's plenty of you to go around."

Even with the banter, Cate could hear the affection between the two and she couldn't help smiling. She hoped to find that for herself one day, the comfort of knowing you were loved and supported and that your person would always be there for you, no matter what.

As if reading her thoughts, Davian squeezed her hand again, his blue eyes glowing with encouragement. Once upon a time, she'd thought Davian was her person. Then he'd disappeared. Now that he was back again, she was fighting to remember not to trust him, but after the past few days it was getting harder and harder to remember exactly why she shouldn't.

"Where is your daughter's father, Dr. Neves?" the King asked out of the blue, knocking Cate right out of her fuzzy warm thoughts regarding Davian and straight back to reality.

"Oh. Uh…" She swallowed the last bite of her first course and kept her eyes down as Noah cleared her plate. The last thing she wanted was for the crew to get ideas about her and Davian and start spreading that around. Bad enough Carrie in the clinic pored over those stupid tabloid rags about the royals. Cate took a sip of water, considering her answer carefully. "He's not part of the picture at present."

Not a total lie. Not the complete truth either.

Beside her, Cate felt Davian tense and he pushed his plate away half-finished.

"Perhaps, Father," Davian said, his voice edged sharply, "we could discuss something other than Cate's personal life."

"Why?" King Phillipe countered. "When that is the elephant in the room?"

"Father!" Davian said at the same time his mother said, "Phillipe!"

"What?" The King shrugged. "I just like to get things out in the open is all."

Oh, God.

Cate looked at Davian, blood pounding in her ears. They'd talked about this. They'd decided together that they wouldn't tell anyone about Adella being his daughter yet. Not until they'd worked out all the logistics of coparenting. But what if he'd gone ahead and told his parents anyway? What if…

This was exactly why Cate didn't trust people. This was exactly why—

"Out in the open?" Davian's voice went cold as ice. "I think you mean cover things up, don't you? That's what you always used me for, isn't it? To deflect attention away from the things you'd rather not have seen or discussed, Father? That is in no way getting things out in the open." His mother gasped, and Cate held his hand tighter, trying to get him to stop and sit down. This wasn't the time or place to have an argument. But it seemed that Davian took after his father in more ways than looks, because the next thing Cate knew, both men had stood and were facing off across the table, while the two women looked on, wide-eyed and horrified. "So do not speak to me of openness and truth, Father. And what elephant is it you speak of here?"

"I'm trying to protect our family's reputation, son," his father said, not backing down an inch. "That's all I've ever tried to do. Protect this family. And look at what it's gotten me. A bad heart, death threats and our names splashed over every cheap newspaper in the world." His dark, intense gaze moved from Davian to Cate. "So, Dr. Neves. I ask you point-blank. What is your interest in my son? Are you being paid to get information from him? It seems rather convenient that you'd reappear in his life on board this ship so suddenly after five years. And what a coincidence that that's the exact age of your daughter as well. Are you trying to blackmail him? How can you possibly trust this woman, Davian? I taught you better than that."

Stunned speechless, Cate looked from the King to the Queen, to Davian, to finally Noah, who still stood near the wall, his face impassive even though he must've heard the fight going on. How could he not, with the King bellowing?

This was her worst nightmare come true. Her personal business, the thing she'd worked so hard to get past in her life, rising to consume her now. She should have never taken this charter in the first place. She should have gone back to Boston and continued with her plans to open her clinic. That would've been the smart choice. The safe choice.

But then I'd never have seen Davian again...

And much as she wanted to deny it, she'd missed him. More than she ever thought possible. The brief time they'd spent together aboard the *Querencia* the past week, and today in Monaco, it was like they'd taken up right where they'd left off five years ago. Easy. Comfortable. Right. Like two halves of one whole. And

Adella adored him too. How could she have missed that?

Before she could say anything though, Davian squared his broad shoulders beneath his expensive tailored charcoal-gray suit and rode to her defense, just like the white knight in a fairy tale, his face tight and his gaze bright with suppressed emotion. "First of all, Father, I trust Cate implicitly. She has been steadfast and supportive and always there when I needed her, no matter the situation. She is an excellent physician and a good friend. She has never once betrayed me, even after I did so to her. There is no one on earth I trust more." He inhaled deep through his nose, ignoring the King's disgruntled snort. "Second, I'm tired of living my life on a maybe. Maybe this person is bad. Maybe this person is lying. Maybe this person will hurt me. Who knows? Maybe they will. But you can't go through life expecting the worst. And I refuse to do it anymore. Not for you, not for the family, not for anyone."

"Now, see here, son—" his father started, but Davian cut him off.

"No, you see here, Father." Davian tugged on Cate's hand until she stood beside him. He looked over at her and whispered, "Trust me?"

Despite the past, despite the tiny alarms going off in the back of her head, right then and there—

tonight—she did trust him. Cate nodded, heart pounding and throat dry as bone.

Davian gave a small nod then turned back to his parents. His father had moved closer to his mother now, his hand on her shoulder, as if for support. Davian looked between the two of them then said, "Cate and I were involved back in college. Romantically. The night you called me home to Ruclecia, we made love for the first time. We've rekindled our relationship now. And plan to continue doing so, regardless of your objections."

Oh, boy.

She waited for him to drop the rest of the bombshell. This was not how Cate had intended for them to find out about Adella, but now that he seemed intent on going there, she had no way of pulling Davian back. Thankfully, Davian had slid his arm around her waist because her knees were wobbling so much Cate thought she might collapse otherwise. She'd worked through life-threatening medical emergencies that were less stressful than this.

Except…he said instead, "Adella is a wonderful little girl. Smart, funny, kind, inquisitive. Any father would be proud to have her as his child and any family would be lucky to have her. Please do not ever let me hear you disparage her or her mother again. I've missed five years with Cate, and I don't intend to miss any more while I'm here. There are no ulterior motives behind Cate and Adella's appearance now. They are close friends of mine and therefore have my protection. Is that understood?"

"But what about the tabloids?" the King blustered. "What about the threats in Ruclecia?"

"What about them?" Davian stood firm. "I'm aware of the dangers we face, Father. But I refuse to let them rule my life any longer. We have the best security team available, both back home and here on the yacht, and there's nothing more we could ask for. I'm not the Crown Prince. My brother has trained his whole life for that position, and he will rule Ruclecia well. Please allow me to live the life that I've trained for as a doctor and stop using me as a pawn in your royal games."

The two men eyed each other across the table, the air taut with tension, until finally Davian's mother cleared her throat delicately.

"Perhaps we should continue dinner now? Two raviolis, no matter how delicious, won't keep me from starving tonight."

Her touch of humor broke the intense bubble they found themselves in and everyone could breathe again. Davian helped Cate back into her seat before taking his own once more. The King sat also, his cheeks a bit ruddier from the exchange with his son, but he let his line of questioning go, staying mainly silent the rest of the meal, while Cate and Davian and his mother discussed their day in Monaco and the weather on the cruise.

Noah, being the excellent steward he was, never showed any sign of hearing a word of the argument that had happened in front of him, just continued to serve the chef's amazing dinner. For the second course, they had flowery spring sushi with Alentejo olive oil, followed by a spring fricassee with Ciflorette strawberries, broad beans, Selma fennel and gourmet peas for the third course, white asparagus from Laigné-en-Belin browned in salted butter for the fourth, and spring cabbage stuffed with fresh garlic Thermidrome with Parmigiano-Reggiano for the fifth. For the sixth main course, the chef made aiguillette of midnight blue lobster with Côtes du Jura and fondant potatoes and finished it all up with a final trio of sweets—profiteroles glazed with verbena, all-flower honey soufflé, and crispy mille-feuille.

"Ah, such a wonderful dinner," the Queen said to Noah as he cleared her plates. "Please give the chef our sincere thanks for his skills tonight."

"Of course, Your Majesty," Noah said, bowing. "I'm so glad you enjoyed it."

Once the table had been cleared, Noah and

another steward came around with coffees and champagne. Davian's parents, however, declined both.

"We're going back to our cabin," the King said. "Please excuse us."

"Father, I—" Davian started.

"No, son. You made yourself quite clear earlier. No need to say any more." The King met Cate's gaze and gave a curt nod. "Glad to have finally met you, Dr. Neves."

"Same, Your Majesty," she said, dropping one more awkward curtsy.

"Don't worry about him," the Queen said, coming around the table to hug and kiss Davian. "He'll adjust, as he always does. Just give him time."

Then she moved to hug and kiss Cate as well. She was so astonished, she stood like a statue as the Queen embraced her. "It really was lovely to meet you, dear. I can tell how happy you make my youngest son and he deserves that so much. I'm glad you're here."

The royal couple then glided away back downstairs to the master suite in a swirl of lilac-scented perfume and pomp, leaving Cate feeling both bewildered and bewitched by it all.

"Wow. That was…" she mumbled.

"Yes, it was," Davian agreed. "I'm sorry about my father. He goes over the top sometimes."

"He cares about you and wants you to be safe, that's all," Cate said, being diplomatic.

"Right." Davian grabbed two champagne flutes off the table and handed one to Cate, then led her upstairs to the top deck to sit and relax. Once they settled on the comfy, oversize love seat, Cate toed off her shoes and tucked her feet under her. Davian took off his suit jacket and draped it over the back of the seat, then took off his shoes as well. He took a long swig of champagne and stared out into the night, his handsome face carved in moonlight. "What my father cares about most is maintaining the family reputation. The royal destiny."

"How so? If you're talking about the tabloids, well, that's been going on for years…"

"No. More than that. He's very old-school. Always has been. To him, it's all about the succession of the crown. I mean, my parents love me. I know that. And I never lacked for anything in my life, but I also knew that I was lower on the list of importance, title-wise."

"Because your brother is the Crown Prince."

"Yes, exactly."

Cate frowned. "Do you resent him for that?"

"No, not at all!" Davian sounded adamant. "I love Arthur and I meant what I said earlier to my father. He's trained hard to be King and will make an excellent ruler someday. But that doesn't mean that I don't have my own goals and dreams outside of the royal family as well."

"Of course." Cate sipped her champagne. The bubbles tickled her nose and on top of the wine she'd had at dinner, the alcohol was creating a nice little buzz inside her. "That's why you went to medical school."

"Exactly." He looked over at her now, smiling, and the effect was devastatingly sexy. Their knees brushed on the love seat and awareness shimmered through her bloodstream. "And that's why I started my charity and my hospital. To make a name for myself outside of my title and my family. To make a real mark on the world outside of money and privilege. To give back." He sighed and closed his eyes. "But my father has a restricted view of what royals should and should not do and be. He doesn't feel I need a career outside of the family business, and he worries about the threats made against us as well. It took years of convincing for him to let me go to America for medical school, and even then I had a full security detail and Grigorio with me to report back to my father regularly. All that pressure, all that responsibility. It's been like a cage around me my whole life. Trapping me inside."

"I'm sorry," Cate said, placing her hand on his leg to comfort him. "That must be very hard for you."

Davian put his hand over hers on his knee and entwined their fingers, then downed the rest of his champagne with one gulp.

"Well," she said, finishing her own champagne then setting the glass aside on the floor next to his. "I enjoyed meeting them tonight anyway. You probably don't want to hear this, but you look a lot like your father." Davian groaned and she laughed. "But you have your mother's eyes. And she is a sweetheart."

"She really is." He had an elbow on the back of the love seat and rested his cheek in his hand, grinning. Then he let go of Cate's other hand and placed his palm on her bare calf, slowly massaging the muscle there, relaxing her even more. "And so are you. You handled them both brilliantly tonight. Especially my father. When I saw him interrogating you like that, Cate, I wanted to dive across the table at him."

"I can handle myself," she said, moving her legs slightly so her toes brushed the side of his thigh. "But I appreciate your support. And I also appreciate you not telling them everything about Adella too. For a moment there, I was scared. Wasn't sure I could trust you."

"Hmm." Davian moved closer on the love seat, pulling Cate's legs across his lap, and causing the skirt of her dress to ride higher, exposing more of her tanned skin to him. His fingers traced higher up her leg, to the outside of her thigh, making her shiver in the warm night. Stars twinkled above them, and it all felt magical. "You can, you know."

"What?" she asked, frowning, her mind moving a bit slower from the champagne and wine.

"Trust me," he said, scooting closer still, his hand on her hip now. "I never wanted to hurt you, Cate. I hope you can believe me now."

Cate narrowed her gaze in the moonlight, reaching out her hand to trace her fingers down his cheek and neck to the top of his tie, loosening it then undoing the button beneath. None of this felt real, yet every nerve in her body felt hyperaware of him. She wasn't sure where life would take them after this charter, or what would happen with them and Adella, but she was sure of one thing. She wanted Davian. And tonight, she'd have him.

Before he could react, she tugged him to her by his tie and kissed him soundly. Davian groaned low in his throat, his fingers digging into her hip through her dress, moving her closer still, as his other hand slid into her hair, keeping her mouth on his as he pulled her completely onto his lap to straddle him.

It felt like a switch had been flipped inside Cate then and she couldn't get enough.

Eventually, Davian pulled away slightly, both

of them breathless as he met her gaze in the moonlight. "Come to my cabin, Cate. Please. I don't want this night to end. Not yet."

She watched him a long moment, her whole being pulsing for his, then raised a hand to trace her fingers down his cheek, making him shiver. An answering yearning lit his eyes, making her pulse notch higher and her blood sing. "I don't want it to end either, Davian. Let's go."

They kissed as he picked her up and carried her down the stairs. For a quick second, Cate worried about the crew seeing them like this, since she still had to work with them for the rest of the charter, but they didn't encounter anyone on the way belowdecks, thankfully. And once Davian began nuzzling her neck and she had her legs wrapped around his waist, she stopped caring about everything but him anyway.

They made their way down the hall to his stateroom, still not breaking the kiss. Once inside, they discarded their clothes in a fast flurry, then fell naked onto his bed, neither able to stop touching and stroking and tasting the other, bolder now than the first time they'd been together, but then they were five years older now too. Back then it had been more tentative, all about exploring, getting to know what the other liked. Now it was hot and intense, making every touch, every sigh more meaningful.

Davian kissed his way down to her breasts, cupping them in his palms then taking one taut nipple into his mouth. Cate arched into him, crying out, her need for him shooting like lightning straight between her legs. She pulled him closer, needing more, and Davian gave her everything, putting all his emotions into his caresses. This was more than sex for her. Way more. It always had been with Davian. To Cate, they were making love in every sense of the word.

Davian thought he'd died and gone to heaven when Cate turned the tables on him, kissing her way down his body to his abdomen, then lower still, tracing her tongue over the tip of his erection. While Davian was an experienced man, being with Cate was different from any lover he'd had before. Always had been. Even that first time together, all those years ago. But before, he'd felt heated and rushed and inquisitive, still learning how to please her. Now he knew Cate better and it seemed to shed a new light on their lovemaking. He knew what she liked, knew how to make her comfortable and happy and satisfied before he took his own pleasure. When the attention of her lips and tongue on his most sensitive flesh grew to be too much for him to bear much longer, he pulled her away to kiss her before turning them over, so Cate was on her back beneath him. Then he kissed and nuzzled his way down her body, wanting to return the favor for her, to make love to her with his hands and mouth until she tumbled over the brink into orgasm, unable to keep from whispering his name over and over as the waves of ecstasy rocked her entire being.

At last, he rose above her, reaching into his nightstand drawer for a condom. They gazes met as he put it on, then positioned himself at her wet entrance. Then she reached down between them again, encircling his hard length, stroking him until Davian pulled her hand away and kissed her palm. "Too much of that, darling, and I won't last."

In answer, Cate drew him down for an open-mouthed kiss, pressing her body to his. "Please, my prince. I need you…"

Hearing his title on her lips nearly drove him over the edge again. But Davian summoned his willpower and held his weight on his forearms, the tip of his hard length poised to enter her. He wanted tonight to last. To be so hot and so good, it was seared into both their memories for eternity. A beat passed, then two, before he finally entered her in one long stroke, then held still, allowing Cate's body to adjust to his. When he did move at last, they both moaned deeply, and he began a rhythm that had them teetering on the brink in no time at all.

"Davian, I…" Cate cried out as she climaxed once more, her words lost as the pleasure overtook her. Davian was close behind. Maybe it was finding each other again after all this time. Maybe it was the moonlight. Maybe it was how they were still so in sync, even after all this time, that set Davian's nerve endings on fire and rocked his foundations. Whatever it was, being inside her felt like a live wire, sparking and shimmering with pleasure. He drove into her once, twice more, wanting it to last forever, but knowing it would be over too soon. Then his body tightened, and he came hard inside Cate, his face buried in her neck and her name on his lips, murmuring sweet nothings into the side of her neck.

Afterward, they lay in the darkness, listening to the sound of the waves outside, gently lapping against the side of the yacht, his head resting in the valley between her breasts, over Cate's heart, and her fingers in his hair, tracing lazy circles against his scalp. Davian felt sated and relaxed for the first time in recent memory and he had his Cate to thank for that as well. "That… Wow," he said, his voice quiet in the shadows. "I don't know what this is between us, but it's still there. And I'm not ready to let it go yet."

"Agreed."

He moved to look up at her, but couldn't really see her face in the shadows, but the vulnerability in her tone made his heart clench. He wanted to explore the possibilities, try to find a workable way to be together as a family, even if it scared them. Davian rolled over onto his back and pulled Cate into his side, her leg sprawling across his and her head on his chest as he pulled the covers up over them and gathered her close. "You know, I came on this yacht to protect my parents, but it seems we're continuing our own journey now. History is repeating itself." He sighed, hesitated. "I only ever wanted to protect you, Cate. And now Adella too. To have a family of my own. A life of my own. Perhaps we can make that together, you and I."

"Perhaps," she whispered, her tone bittersweet, and Davian's chest tightened.

He knew this was tender territory for her, after what happened with her father. He knew she didn't trust easily. Neither did he. But he was willing to try, for Cate. For their daughter. Still, he didn't want to ruin this moment, this one perfect evening together, so he kept that to himself. They'd have plenty of time to talk about it tomorrow.

"Let's get some sleep," he said, his words buried in her hair, warm and deep as he nestled

Cate's head under his chin, and she snuggled closer into his heat. "Sweet dreams, Cate."

"Sweet dreams, my prince," Cate said, kissing his chest before they both drifted off to slumber.

CHAPTER TEN

EARLY THE NEXT MORNING, Cate was back in the clinic, still reeling a bit from her night with Davian. Her body ached in interesting ways when she moved around the exam room and her heart felt full. She'd awakened before dawn and left a sleeping Davian in bed, giving him a soft kiss on the cheek before sneaking back to her own cabin for a shower and change of clothes. Then she'd picked up Adella at Carrie's cabin and taken her daughter to breakfast in the crew cafeteria before work.

"Did you have a sleepover last night, Mommy?" Adella asked, milk from her cereal dripping down her chin. "You won't let me have sleepovers."

Cate grabbed a napkin to clean up Adella's chin, her face prickling with embarrassment. "That's because you're five."

"So, when I'm older, I can have sleepovers like you?"

"No," Cate said quickly, frowning down at

her plate of toast. "I mean, yes. I mean, Mommy didn't have a sleepover, sweetie. I was just up late talking to a friend, that's all."

"Uh-huh," Noah said, coming over to sit at their table. "Is that what they're calling it now?"

Great. Just when she thought she'd escaped the prying eyes of her cocrew. She should've known better. The life of a yachtie didn't exactly lend itself to privacy. Cate picked up her coffee and scowled over the rim at her friend. Noah grinned, ignoring her pointed suggestion for him to change subjects. "So, how was dinner with the Prince last night?"

"You ate with the King and Queen!" Adella clapped her hands. "Did you get to wear a crown too?"

"No." Cate set her mug down and pushed her toast away. Any appetite she'd had was now gone under the realization that yep, she'd slept with Davian again last night. Not that she hadn't been a willing and enthusiastic participant at the time, but now in the light of day, the ramifications of that were starting to sink in.

I only ever wanted to protect you, Cate. And now Adella too. To have a family of my own. A life of my own. Perhaps we can make that together, you and me...

Together.

You and me.

Oh, Lord.

Cate realized her daughter and Noah were both looking at her expectantly, so she added, "No crowns. Just fancy food and conversation."

"Mmm. More like interrogation," Noah said.

He wasn't wrong. Cate had expected his parents to be curious about her, but she hadn't expected the third degree. It had been a bit unsettling, on top of the stress of meeting royalty, and had set her back a step. Thankfully, Davian had been there to support her. That was nice, knowing someone had her back. He'd been that way in residency too, and she'd missed that about him. Among other things.

Okay, fine. She'd missed pretty much everything about him.

Which was a serious problem.

Cate didn't want to miss him. Didn't want to need anyone. Because people let you down.

"Mommy, isn't that your face?" Adella asked, pointing at the newspaper another crew member was reading at the table.

Cate glanced behind her to see what her daughter was pointing at and nearly fell out of her chair.

"Oh, my God!" Noah gasped. "That is you."

He got up and walked over the table and asked to see the paper then brought it back to Cate. It was one of the local gossip sheets the crew member had picked up in Monaco before they'd left port early that morning. Noah sat back down and held up the front page.

The headline made Cate's stomach knot. "Passionate Prince Hooks Up with Ship Doc."

Adella had abandoned her soggy cereal and was gawking at the selfie Cate had taken near the Albert statue of her and Davian before they sat down to rest. And kiss. And, oh, my God indeed! She swallowed hard and grabbed the paper away from Noah and stared down at it, her own smiling face mocking her from the tabloid. "How in the world did they get this shot? I took it on my personal phone."

"Paparazzi?" Noah suggested, squinting at the picture. "You look cute though. Both of you. And look at Adella, sleeping in the stroller like a baby. So cute!"

"I'm not a baby!" Adella said, crossing her arms and pouting. "Mommy, tell him I'm not a baby!"

"She's not a baby," Cate murmured without really paying much attention. This was bad. She felt violated, taken advantage of by some unknown photographer. But no. Looking closer at the picture, there was no way someone else had taken this shot. It was identical to the one on her phone. So how in the world... Then she read the article and it went from bad to worse.

The reporter, if you could call them that, cited an anonymous source who remarked on how much Adella resembled Davian. The hair, the eyes, even her little expressions sometimes. All Davian, through and through.

Cate stood quickly, nearly knocking over her chair in her haste. "I need to go. Noah, can you watch Adella for me for a bit, please?"

"Uh, yeah. Sure." He frowned at her. "Everything okay?"

"No, it really isn't," she said. "Be good, sweetie. Mommy loves you."

Cate rushed out of the cafeteria and headed up toward the guest staterooms intent on talking to Davian about the article immediately. But when he answered her knock on his door, he was already on the phone with someone, and from his tight expression, the conversation wasn't going well.

He waved her inside then closed the door and held up a finger for her to wait.

"Hang on, Arthur. What are you saying? How is that possible?"

Her mind kept whirling, her old fears creeping up again. There were only the two of them in Monaco yesterday. If she didn't send those photos to the press then who did? Davian? His family?

She didn't want to believe that, but he'd told

her himself how devious his family had been in manipulating the press to their whims. Would they try to use Cate and Adella as their pawns now? To throw the press off the King's health issues?

Cate hated to believe that, but with only the two of them there, it was hard to find another explanation for the leak.

No. Stop.

Maybe this was just another coping mechanism. Another way to keep herself guarded because she was falling for Davian all over again. She didn't want to get hurt. Didn't want to open her heart to him and be vulnerable when their future was so uncertain.

Unfortunately, Cate was confused and confounded and feared it wouldn't get better any time soon.

"I'm telling you what I'm seeing, brother," the Crown Prince said into the phone. "It's all over the tabloids here in Ruclecia. Which means it's all over everywhere else too."

Dammit.

Davian had thought he'd been so careful yesterday, so careful with this charter, but apparently not. He looked over at Cate and spotted the paper under her arm. His stomach dropped to his toes. Yep, she'd seen it too. He walked over and held out his hand for the paper and she gave it to him.

In bold, bright colors across the front page were their faces, happy and smiling in Monaco. Given that they'd been about to kiss, it could've been worse, though he wasn't in a forgiving mood now.

"I need to go, Arthur," Davian said. "I'll call you back."

"Wait!" his brother shouted. "Be careful with telling Father. You know how upset he gets."

"I know. And I will."

He ended the call then stalked over to Cate, skimming the article on the way. Nothing too detailed, thank goodness, though there were speculations made about Adella and her resemblance to Davian. His chest burned hotter. It was one thing for the press to go after him. It was another to involve an innocent child.

My innocent child.

"I'm afraid they're going to connect the dots between all of this, Davian," Cate said, looking pale and fraught. "This is exactly what I didn't want to happen. Not until we've figured things out ourselves. Told Adella."

"Same." He slumped down onto the sofa and scrubbed a hand over his face. He'd showered but hadn't had a chance to shave yet. Hell, he still only had on a towel around his waist. Still, he was glad Cate was there so they could get to the bottom of this. "How did they get this photo?"

"That's what I can't figure out." Cate took the paper back from him to stare at the photo again. "At first, I thought it was paparazzi, but this is a selfie from my phone, Davian. Which means someone must've hacked into it."

"But how?" He scowled. "It is password-protected and encrypted, yes?"

"Yes." She sighed and sat back. "I've no idea how they do any of that, but I do know they get better at breaking into things every day. Oh, God." Cate closed her eyes and tipped her head back. "What are we going to do? I mean, I don't care so much for myself, but I don't want Adella involved. And what about your father?"

Davian took her hand and exhaled slow. "My brother said the picture and article are already making the news circuit, but hopefully being at sea today will keep my father from finding out until I can decide how best to tell him."

"Well, at least it wasn't too scandalous. He knew we were going into Monaco, so it's not totally out of the realm of possibility that someone might see us and snap a photo."

"True." Davian shook his head. "But he will be upset and blame me anyway, because that's what he does."

"I'm sorry." She leaned her head on his shoulder then straightened fast. "And please know I had nothing to do with this, Davian. I swear to you."

"I believe you." He kissed her cheek then rested his cheek against the top of her head as she relaxed it on his shoulder again. "We'll figure it out. But let me finish getting dressed first."

While he did that, Cate scrolled through her phone, checking emails, and searching for any more information about their visit that had been released to the press. By the time Davian was done getting ready and was back by her side on the sofa, she'd found a dozen articles—all speculating about their relationship and about Adella's parentage.

"Davian, what are we going to do? According to the number of search engine hits this has, the story is going viral."

"Let me make some calls."

Davian stood and paced his stateroom as he talked with the IT security team back in Ruclecia. They took all the information from him and from Cate's phone to try to track how the photo had been hacked. He next talked to the palace PR team and put them on disaster mode, having them arrange a different departure point for the private jet that would take his parents back to Ruclecia so they wouldn't be mobbed at their arrival at the island of Corsica. They had originally planned to sail on to Sicily before ending their charter, but with all this nonsense, it was probably better to return early.

Once that was finished, he returned to Cate. "We should go up and speak to my father before he finds out about this elsewhere. Come."

He took her hand and helped her up then led her to the door. As soon as Davian opened it though, his father stood there, red-faced and fuming angry, glaring at them.

"I told you this would happen," his father spat out, pointing at Cate. "I told you not to trust her."

Davian thrust Cate behind him, keeping himself between her and his father. He was used to these outbursts. Cate was not. "This is not her fault, Father. Her phone was hacked."

"Hacked? Is that what she told you?"

"Yes. And I believe her."

His father sputtered a moment and Davian feared he might have another coronary right there in the hall.

"Please, Father. Calm down. I've already got the palace on alert and the IT security team is looking into it. It's all handled. And Arthur called me first thing. We've got this under control."

"These insidious rumors are never under control once they start, Davian. You know that."

"Then we will deal with the fires as they come

up." Davian had felt Cate tense behind him and wanted to shield her as best he could from his father's anger. Lord knew he'd been the brunt of it enough growing up and it could be brutal. "Please, Father. Let's go upstairs and have a nice breakfast. Forget about this nonsense. I've contacted the jet pilot and have arranged for them to pick us up the day after tomorrow in Corsica. All is well, I promise. Don't concern yourself over this."

"Don't concern myself?" he continued to bluster as Davian herded the King down the hall toward the stairs. "How exactly am I supposed to do that when the press is speculating that this woman's child is yours, Davian? I can't have people running around calling every bastard on the planet part of my family. How much did they pay you for the pictures? I hope it was worth it."

"Hey!" Cate shouted sternly from behind Davian. "My daughter is not a bastard. Don't you ever call her that again. You'd be lucky to have her in your family. And for your information, I—"

"Father, stop," Davian commanded, cutting her off, for what little good it did. His father continued grumbling and climbing up to the deck anyway. "Don't say things you'll regret."

They stepped out into the sunshine when his father rounded on Davian, his dark eyes hard.

"The only thing I regret, Davian, is that you can't be more like your brother. At least he does his duty for this family."

Only years of swallowing his emotions kept Davian from lashing out then. He squeezed his fists tight, so tight that Cate gasped and pulled free of him. Still, something of his outrage must've shown on his face because his father took a step back, apparently knowing he'd gone too far. Lips tight, Davian managed to grind out, "My whole life, all I've ever been about is duty to this family, Father."

The King took another step back, the color draining from his face before he turned and walked away.

CHAPTER ELEVEN

INSTEAD OF IMPROVING, Davian's frustrations only worsened.

The palace IT security team had spent the better part of the day investigating the leaked photos from Cate's phone and had traced their sending back to the yacht itself, meaning someone on board the *Querencia* had sent them to the press. And not just any crew either. The transmission signal for the email could be tracked to the area where the medical clinic was located.

A black hole had opened in Davian's gut at that news. He left the abominably hot galley and went back upstairs to the top deck from some fresh air. In his heart of hearts, he never wanted to believe that Cate had been involved in the leak at all. It was ridiculous. Absurd. She had absolutely nothing to gain by having those photos appear in the press and everything to lose.

Except money...

No. He shook off the sound of his father's

voice in his head. Cate did not need money. Having seen the budget himself for this charter, he knew all the crew were well compensated for their work here. And if there was anything she needed, Cate knew all she had to do was ask him, right? She was starting her own clinic, which wasn't cheap, but she was also smart and resourceful and had told him she'd been planning for the project for a while now, so that meant she had funding secured, didn't it?

How much did they pay you for the pictures? I hope it was worth it.

Cursing under his breath, Davian leaned on the railing and stared out over the turquoise water of the Mediterranean. They'd started this trip with so much hope, and yesterday in Monaco had been so delightful, but now the bright sunshine seemed to mock him. Davian was tired, so very tired of cleaning up other people's messes, of always being on guard, of the constant scrutiny, of never measuring up in his father's eyes, despite his best efforts. He wanted to just live his life, run his hospital, help people, cure diseases, be happy, start a family of his own, be a good father to Adella and support Cate in whatever way she'd let him.

Cate.

He hung his head and closed his eyes behind his sunglasses. The winds were stronger today, blowing the linen shirt he wore around his torso and tousling his hair. The scent of salt and sea and suspicions surrounded him, churning his emotions into a tangled mess.

There were only three people in the clinic for this charter. Dr. Bryant, who'd been a trusted mentor to Davian for years and was above reproach in this whole situation. Hell, given the man's age and the fact he'd never even seen him use a cell phone, Davian wasn't even sure the man owned one, let alone had the technical skills to leak photos to someone without getting caught. Which left Cate and the receptionist, Carrie.

He doubted the receptionist would have done it, given that she was in her cabin the whole night watching Adella while he and Cate had dinner with his parents then went back to Davian's stateroom afterward. And the IT team had specifically traced the signal to the clinic area of the ship. It made no sense. The tension in his gut tightened. Thinking logically, if the receptionist had been eliminated, then the potential for it to be Cate increased and…

No. Absolutely not.

Davian refused to believe Cate had anything to do with this. She'd vehemently denied it at the time and had been as shocked as he was about the leak. She'd taken measures from the time she'd discovered Davian was on board the *Querencia* to shield their daughter from any hint of scandal. It made no sense for her to blow all that up for a few thousand dollars, or whatever amount the paparazzi were paying for photos of the Ruclecian royals these days.

Maybe it's payback...

Payback? He wasn't sure where that had come from, but it had him sitting down as his knees buckled. They'd had this conversation. She'd accepted his explanation about why he'd left so quickly back in residency. She'd said she understood his reasons and forgave him. And she'd been keeping a huge secret of her own from him. They were both guilty there. Cate would never use that against him. She knew that would gut him. She knew how he felt about her, how he'd always felt about her. She was the only person he'd ever loved, ever allowed inside, ever been truly vulnerable with.

He couldn't, wouldn't accept that it was Cate behind all this.

But if not her, who?

Enough. Enough guessing and speculation. Time to have the difficult conversation and get it all out there. Only then would he know the truth. Davian stood and headed back downstairs to the clinic to find Cate.

* * *

"I just can't figure out how that picture got from my phone to the press," Cate said, as she sorted files in the clinic. "I had my phone with me all day. It's not like I left it somewhere and a stranger accessed it or anything."

"It is weird," Carrie said from the reception desk, where she was looking at said photo online. "But it's not the end of the world, right? And you all look amazing in the picture, so there's that."

Cate gave the younger woman a look. "Seriously? That's the last thing I care about here. My privacy was invaded, Carrie. I didn't show those photos to anyone. The only reason I took them was to have memories of our day yesterday to look back on once I'm in Boston again." Cate shuddered and closed the file cabinet drawer. "To think someone close enough to me to take my phone did that to me. I feel so violated."

Carrie turned away to continue reading the article while Cate continued to stew to herself. "I mean, who would do that? It's awful, taking advantage of people like that. I can understand why now Davian's family detests the paparazzi so much. And poor Adella. She's just an innocent child in all this. It was my duty to protect her, and I failed as a mother." She covered her face with her hands and sighed. "I've failed her all around here. I'm a failure."

"Mommy?" Adella said from where she was playing with her toys in a corner of the clinic. "What's a failure?"

Me, Cate wanted to say, but held back. She took a deep breath and walked over to crouch beside Adella. "It's when someone doesn't get the outcome they wanted, or things don't end up the way you wanted them, sweetie. It's a part of life, but it can hurt sometimes."

"I'm sorry, Mommy," Adella said, reaching up to pat Cate's cheek. "But I still love you."

"I love you too, sweetie." She pulled her little girl into a hug. "More than I can every say."

They were still like that when Davian arrived at the clinic. He walked in and headed straight to Carrie's desk, apparently not seeing Cate and Adella off to the side.

Carrie looked up then did a double take, nearly falling out of her chair to get up and curtsy before Davian. "Your Highness, good morning. How can the clinic help you today?"

"I need to see Dr. Neves," he said. "It's urgent."

"I'm here," Cate said, pulling back from Adella. She straightened and pointed to Dr. Bryant's office. "We can go in here for privacy. He's not working today."

They went into the office and Cate closed the door behind them before Davian took her into his arms and held her tight. He whispered into her temple, "How are you holding up?"

"Okay." She shrugged and leaned back to meet his gaze. He looked about as rumpled and unsettled as she felt, his shirt and shorts wrinkled and his hair disheveled. Davian had probably been up on deck since he carried the scent of warm sun and salt on his skin. "Just still trying to figure out how all this happened." Cate smoothed a hand down the front of her white medical uniform pants then leaned her hips back against Dr. Bryant's desk. "Have you heard anything from your IT team at the palace?"

He gave a curt nod, staring down at his phone screen and not at her. "They were able to trace the email transmission to on board the ship."

"Oh, wow." Cate frowned and straightened, walking over to peer at his phone too. "Any more details than that?"

"Yes." Davian shut off his phone before she could get a good look at the information there and shoved it into his pocket. "Apparently, it was sent from right here in the clinic."

"What?" She took a step back, as if she'd been struck. "But that can't be right. I was never here last night, Davian. I went right to my cabin after we returned to the *Querencia*. You know that because you walked me here. Then I showered and changed and took Adella to Carrie for her to babysit last night. I was running late so I hurried from there up to the main salon for dinner. And you and I were together after that, so…"

"I know," he said, exhaling slowly and shaking his head as she walked over to sit in one of the chairs before the desk. "That's what makes no sense to me." He scowled and looked up at her. "And you're sure you had your phone with you the entire time?"

"Of course!" Cate crossed her arms, a sudden chill running through her. "I was on call, so I had to have it in case of an emergency. You know that."

"Hmm."

"'Hmm'?" She didn't mean to be snippy, but the stress was getting to her now and she didn't like the direction this conversation was headed. "What does that mean?"

"I don't know, Cate. All I'm certain of is that the evidence doesn't lie. And the evidence says that your phone was here last night to send that photo to the press."

Her breath whooshed out of her in astonishment. "Wait. You think it was me who did this now?"

"I didn't say that," Davian started.

"That's what you're implying!" Hurt and horror quickly bubbled over into outrage, making her words froth over like a too-full boiling pot.

"We were literally together last night from dinner on, Davian. When exactly did I supposedly have time to send this email?"

"Calm down, Cate. Please. I'm not accusing you of anything. And fighting with me won't help anything."

"It certainly will because you're wrong! I had nothing to do with this. Why would I send that, huh? It goes against everything I want for myself, everything I want for my daughter."

A small muscle ticked in his cheek as he looked away, his voice tight with tension, "Money, perhaps?"

"Money." Cate's eyes widened as realization hit home. He wasn't kidding here. He really thought she'd done this. Searing self-recriminations stabbed her in the chest, making it hard to speak past the constriction in her throat. "You think I did this? Sold you out? Betrayed you for money?"

"No." He began pacing again, his gestures agitated. "I don't know. I just… I'm trying to make sense of this and that's the only reason I can come up with, Cate. You said you were going to open your own clinic after this and that takes funds. I thought you—"

"What? That I'd sell you and your family out for a couple of extra bucks? Well, screw you, Davian. I don't need any extra bucks and I certainly don't need to stand here and take this from you!"

She started toward the door, her eyes burning from unshed tears, but she sure as hell refused to let him see her cry. Not after what he'd put her through back in residency and certainly not now, after the awful things he'd just accused her of. Cate made it as far as the door before Davian took her arm, stopping her.

"Cate, please," he said, his grip gentle but firm. "Don't go like this. Let's talk this out."

"Oh, no. I think you've said more than enough already." She rounded on him then, determined to say her piece before she couldn't anymore. "You made me believe you, Davian. You made me open up and start to trust you again. You made me love you again and then you turn around and accuse me of being nothing but a gold digger, looking for an easy paycheck?" Her face felt hotter than the sun then and her vision blurred with the tears she couldn't hold back any longer. "How dare you!" She angrily swiped the back of her hand over her wet cheeks. "How dare you walk back into my life, into Adella's life, like some white knight on your horse and act like you care about us and like you want to have a future with us, then drop us like a hot potato at the first sign of trouble? We are not playthings, and this is not a game, Davian. I told you that from the start. If you want to be Adella's father, you need to be there through it all—the good, the bad and everything in between. I won't take less, and she deserves nothing less than that." Dammit, this was going off the rails now and her heart ached like it would die and she just wanted to get out of there and take Adella back to their cabin, where she could keep her safe from the world and Davian and all this mess. But first, she wanted to break down his walls a little too, make him hurt like he'd hurt her, make him see that he wasn't above accusation either. Petty? Maybe, but she didn't care at this point. Cate sniffled and raised her chin, meeting Davian's cold blue gaze directly. "And for your information, how do I know it wasn't you who leaked that photo?"

"Me?" Now it was his turn to sound outraged. "How the hell would I do that?"

"No idea. But you were there with me all night. You had access to my phone. And it wouldn't be the first time that a royal leaked information to get what they wanted, would it? You said yourself, Davian, that your family was expert at that. Maybe you decided that you could use this scandal to blackmail your own father to get him to allow you to live the life you want, eh?" She squared her shoulders, taking refuge in her old doubts and fears. Trust had always been her Achilles' heel and now she could see a very good reason why. People always let you down in the end. First her father, now Davian. She was done with letting people hurt her or her daughter like this ever again. Cate could tell her barb had struck deep when Davian paled beneath his tan and the corners of his mouth tightened. Time to go. Cate tugged free and grabbed the door handle, the cool metal a shock against her heated palm. "Goodbye, Davian. I doubt we'll see each other again."

But the scene she opened the door to was a chaotic surprise. Four of the royal guards filled the waiting room, two at the entrance, one standing watch over Adella and the fourth one handcuffing Carrie.

"What's going on?" Cate asked, rushing over to sweep her daughter into her arms.

"Mommy? I'm scared," Adella said, burying her face in Cate's chest.

"Explain yourselves," Davian demanded, stalking out into the room. "Why are you arresting this woman?"

"I'm sorry, Your Highness," Carrie said, tears streaming down her face now. "I never meant to cause any problems."

"Speak!" Davian said to the guard holding on to the receptionist. "Tell me what's going on."

"The head of IT called us, Your Highness," the guard said. "They got more information on the leaked photo. Apparently, it wasn't Dr. Neves's phone that sent the picture, but another device with a very similar IMEI number. IT said since the devices were the same make and model, it was possible that the photo could've been copied wirelessly if the two phones were in close proximity, without Dr. Neves even knowing."

"Oh, my God!" Cate stared at Carrie, still trying to take that in. "Is that what happened? Did you copy my photo, Carrie? When?"

Carrie huffed out a breath, her body trembling slightly as she stared down at the floor. "I didn't think it would be a big deal. I never meant to hurt you or anyone else," she said, between sobs. "The paper contacted me before we sailed. They said they'd pay me well for any pictures or juicy tidbits I might hear while we were on charter. I didn't know that you and Prince Davian would get involved, Dr. Neves. I never thought..." She sighed. "I'm so sorry."

"Why didn't you just tell them no?" Cate asked, walking over with Adella to stand beside Davian.

"By the time I had the pictures, I couldn't. I'd already spent the money they'd paid me on bills back home and I had no way of paying it back." Carrie started crying. "I never meant for any of this to happen, Cate. I swear. You're my friend.

I just needed the money and thought this would be an easy way to get it."

"Take her away," Davian said to the guard, and they led Carrie away in handcuffs.

Cate stood and watched, oddly numb. Her life had gone from heavenly to hellish in the span of twenty-four hours and she had no clue what to do about that. The only thing she was certain of at that point was that things between her and Davian had been broken and she wasn't sure they could ever be fixed again.

Davian turned to her, his expression unreadable. "Cate, I'm…"

"No." She started for the door, Adella clutched tight to her like a shield. "I think we've said everything we need to today, Davian. This is exactly what I wanted to avoid, exactly what I feared the most getting involved with you again, knowing who and what you were." She inhaled deep, her lungs tight with sorrow. "I can't live like this. And I won't put my daughter through it either. The constant hounding by the press, the lack of privacy, no personal life. I can't." Her voice broke and she swallowed hard. "I love you, Davian. I always have. But maybe that isn't enough anymore. I must think of Adella. And if you don't trust me, then…"

"I do trust you, Cate. And I'm thinking of Adella too," he said, striding over to her, his blue gaze shining with earnestness. "I want what's best for all of us. And I love you too." He took a deep breath and looked away. "But I agree. Maybe you should take her away, keep her safe. I obviously can't do it."

"Davian, you—" she started, then stopped because what was the point? His words and actions didn't match. "You say you trust me now, but you don't. What you did in that office showed me that. And without trust, we have nothing, Davian. Not love, not a future. Nothing. None of it will work. I'm sorry."

And with that, she walked away from him, back to her cabin, back to her old life and fears, where she should've stayed to begin with. Perhaps then she would've saved herself a lifetime of pain and heartache over the man she'd loved and lost.

CHAPTER TWELVE

FOR THE REST of the day and evening, Davian steered clear of everyone, needing to work through all the complications in his life and future alone. His whole life had been spent in duty to others. First to his family, then to his patients, and now to Cate and Adella. But now he feared he was at a breaking point, a crossroads, and decisions had to be made.

He had to choose who he wanted to be and who he would protect and cherish above all others going forward—his family, his career, or Cate and Adella. Until now, the first had always taken precedence, but deep inside, Davian knew that wasn't what he wanted for his future. He loved his work as well, but not as much as he loved Cate and Adella.

His family would be fine without him. His brother was strong and ready to ascend to the throne of their country. Yes, he wouldn't have Davian to advise him or to take the fall if things

went sideways, but Arthur was smart and com-
passionate, and he had a wife and children of his
own. He'd find a way through just fine. Davian's
parents? That was more concerning. He knew
they loved him, in their own ways. His mother
was affectionate and kind, if a bit distracted. And
his father, well, the man was used to getting his
own way. Sometimes it felt as if he saw both of
his sons as pawns in a chess game he played to
win. But deep down, Davian believed that his
father did care for them, even if he didn't show
it in the ways Davian wished he would.

The conversation he needed to have with his
parents would be difficult, but necessary. They
would make their choice about what part Davian
would play in their future after he told them his
plans, but his own choice was made. He was
done with royal life.

His parents were in the main salon when he
found them. The King was reading the day's papers and the Queen was doing a crossword puz-
zle. They both looked up when he walked in, still
dressed casually in his shirt and shorts.

"We need to talk," Davian said, taking a seat
at the formal dining table.

His father peered at him over the top of his
newspaper. "You've handled the photo scandal,
I see. Good work, son."

Davian gave him a curt nod, biting back an

I-told-you-so where Cate was concerned. What troubled him most though was the fact he'd let his father convince him that maybe he was right. Maybe Cate had betrayed him, just as he'd feared she would. But that wasn't the case. Cate had been true to him, and he'd doubted her for no other reason than his father's accusations. He refused to ever let that occur again.

Once his parents were seated across from him, Davian came out with it, crisp and clear. "I wanted to tell you today that I'm retiring from royal life, effective immediately."

"What?" the King blustered. "That's unacceptable. I refuse to accept."

"Dear, what's this all about?" his mother asked, her tone concerned. "Is it the doctor? Cate?"

"Yes, she's a part of it, but it's much more than that. This had been building for years."

"Of all the ungrateful…" His father's face grew redder by the second. "This family has done everything for you. Supported you, educated you, fed and clothed you."

"As families are supposed to do."

"Stop this impertinence!" His father pounded a fist on the table, his booming voice reverberating around the room. "I will not hear of any withdrawal or retirement or whatever else you call it from this family, do you understand?"

"What I understand is that I've been used and deceived by this family one too many times, Father." Davian remained calm, his tone low and measured. "For too many occasions, I've been a pawn in a larger game to protect the family and serve my duty to you. I've had my life uprooted and my future jeopardized to deflect attention from whatever scandal or crisis rules the day. But I'm done with that. I have a life of my own now. I have work that I enjoy and people that I love and want to spend my future with. And I do not want any of that to be threatened anymore because of my family ties. So, I hereby withdraw from all titles and duties associated with the House of De Loroso and wish to move forward being a full-time doctor and humanitarian, and perhaps one day, if I'm lucky, a husband and father. Also, you should know that Adella Neves is my child. Cate and I had an affair back in residency and there was a baby born, shortly after I was called back to Ruclecia. Cate tried to contact me, but the palace security turned her away. One more reason I want to leave this life behind. I refuse to ever be separated from my daughter again."

"Oh, my!" His mother gasped, trembling. "Davian, is this true? You have a child? I have a granddaughter?"

His father, the King, took the opposite stance. "How do you know this child is yours? Have you had DNA testing done? If she is a member of the family, that will be required for her to take her rightful place in the lineage. I demand to see the results, proof that what you say is true, Davian. You cannot just—"

At that point, having said what he'd intended to say, Davian rose and pushed he chair in. "Actually, I can, Father. Adella is mine. I love her and Cate. I hope to spend the rest of my life with them if they'll have me. You can choose to accept that, accept them and my decisions, or I can walk out of here and out of your lives forever. I've made my choice. Now you must make yours."

The King and Queen spoke quietly to each other, Davian's mother crying softly and his father's color slowly returning to normal as he comforted his wife. Finally, they turned back to Davian and said in unison, "We accept."

For the first time in a very long time, Davian felt a weight being lifted off him. Things weren't perfect, not yet, but perhaps they would be someday. He smiled at his parents. "Good. Thank you. Now, if you'll excuse me, there's someone I need to speak with."

CHAPTER THIRTEEN

Cate was in her cabin packing up her and Adella's stuff. They had a flight home scheduled for the next day and were staying in a hotel on Corsica that night after debarking the yacht. While Cate filled their suitcases and carry-ons, Adella played with her toys on the bed with Paulo, who was back to his old self again following his head injury scare. The boy still had a couple of stitches that would need to come out in a week or so, but otherwise had made a full recovery. Lord Maybrook was also doing better, though his recovery would take longer due to the severity of his injuries and his age.

All they had left to do now was have the crew line up as the charter guests left the yacht and then it would all be over.

Over.

So much had changed in the span of just a couple of weeks that Cate was still trying to wrap her head around it all. Seeing Davian again. Tell-.

ing him about Adella. Meeting his family. Falling for him all over again.

That last one still scared her, but she kept reminding herself that nothing had been decided and as of right now, things were proceeding as planned. She'd go back to Boston and begin preparations to open her clinic, spend some time with her mother, get Adella scheduled and registered for school in the fall. Try to get on with life without knowing when or if Davian might be a part of their future going forward. Of course, he could be a part of Adella's life if he chose, but he either needed to be all in or all out.

She shook her head.

Silly, really. All of it. Two weeks ago, she'd been fine going it alone. She'd be fine now doing the same. Except deep inside her, she wondered if she still wanted to...

"Attention all crew members, please be on deck in five minutes in dress uniform to say goodbye to our guests."

"Yes, Captain," Cate said into the comm unit clipped to the belt of her white uniform pants, then closed the last suitcase she'd been working on. "Okay, kiddos. We need to go up on deck. Put your toys away and let's go."

Both Adella and Paulo, used to this routine by now, did as she asked, waiting for Cate by the door, where she ushered them out of the cabin and up the stairs to the main deck where the other crew were lining up to receive the Ruclecian royals.

After Cate left Adella and Paulo in a corner to sit quietly while she worked, she took her place in line and waited for the King and Queen to come through. She couldn't help wondering how Davian's talk with them had gone. Considering he'd not found her afterward to let her know suggested not as well as he'd planned.

"Dr. Neves," Queen Arabella said as she stopped before Cate. "Thank you for helping to make our cruise such a pleasure. We hope to see more of both of you in the future."

"Thank you, Your Majesty." Cate curtsied, more smoothly this time, then was surprised when the Queen embraced her.

"Our son told us about you and Adella, and I'm so glad he did," Queen Arabella whispered for Cate's ears only. "We've missed so much time with you and Adella. Please come visit us soon at the palace so we can get to know you both properly and welcome you to the family."

Stunned, Cate blinked at the woman once they pulled apart. "Uh, I… I guess we'll need to discuss that."

"Yes. There is much to discuss in that situation," the King said, looking the opposite of his wife's joyful demeanor. In fact, there was a slight grayish pallor to his complexion that Cate didn't like one bit. If he'd been one of her patients, she'd have ordered him admitted for testing. Still, given all the stress they were all under now, and the fact he wasn't her patient, she let it pass. He would be on a plane home within the hour and would be back under his own physician's care soon. Davian's father hardly needed her intercession at this point. The King stood before her, his posture rigid, and his gaze incisive. "I blame you for what my son is doing. Before we came on this trip, he had his head on straight. He knew his duty and was committed to it. Now he's full of fanciful ideas and ridiculous dreams."

"Phillipe!" Queen Arabella gasped, glancing up at her husband. "This is not the place."

"Father," Davian said, coming up behind the King and giving Cate a conciliatory look. "Mother's right. I'm sure Dr. Neves has things to get done before her departure. We can continue our discussion later by phone or video conference."

An angry vein pulsed near the King's temple and his complexion grew mottled. "Do not dare to tell me my place, either of you. I am the King of Ruclecia, and I will—"

The older man froze in place, his face going ashen before he collapsed onto the deck amid surprised cries and calls from the crew.

Cate and Davian immediately sprang into action as another crew member ran downstairs for the emergency kit and portable ECG and defibrillator.

She moved to the King's head to assess his airway, while Davian checked for a pulse.

"Thready and uneven," he said, scowling down at his father's chest as he opened the man's suit jacket and shirt to expose his chest. "Airway?"

"No discernable breaths. Someone call an ambulance to the dock!"

While another crew member ran to report the emergency, Davian began CPR chest compressions on his father while Cate established a clear and open airway, then asked another crew member to administer oxygen to the King using a bag and mask while she moved to the King's other side to place the patches for the defibrillator machine and turn on the monitor. "Davian, can you stop chest compressions to see what kind of rhythm we have?"

They both stared at the screen.

"Definite defib," Davian said, glancing behind him to where Noah waited to take over CPR when Davian tired. "Okay, let's defibrillate at one hundred and fifty joules, please, and we'll change compressors afterward, yes?"

Noah nodded. "Yes."

"Stand clear," Cate said, turning the dial on the machine to the requested amount then hitting the button. The King's body jerked from the electric jolt. "Shock delivered."

"Okay. Let's continue compressions," Davian said, his voice flat and stoic.

Cate ached for him. This was why doctors never worked on their own family members. Emergencies were high-emotion, high-stress incidents anyway. Add in all the other dynamics and it was far too difficult to be objective about the treatment and the outcome.

Davian took up the oxygen delivery once Noah took over on the CPR. "We can handle this. You should see about your mother."

"No. She's fine." He glanced over to where the captain was comforting the Queen. "I need to do this. It's my fault this happened."

"This isn't your fault," Cate said. "You said yourself your father's been in poor health. He recently had bypass surgery and has a history of cardiac problems. None of this now is your fault."

"I shouldn't have talked to him about leaving my royal duties. I should have waited until we were home," he said, his gaze locked on his father's grayish face. "I should have—"

"Stop." Cate kept her tone firm but quiet. "Second-guessing yourself now doesn't do anyone any good. If you'd waited, then something else would've come up, preventing you from telling him again. You did what you did because you had to, Davian. Living a lie hurts everyone involved. Believe me, I know." She drew up one milligram of epinephrine into a syringe then injected it into a vein in the King's arm. "Administering meds now."

After Cate disposed of the used syringe, Davian looked up at the monitor again. "Still in defib."

"Ambulance on the way," the crew member said, returning.

"Good." Cate checked her watch again. "Okay. It's been two minutes since the last shock. Let's stop compressions and reassess his rhythm again."

Noah lifted his hands away from the King's chest.

"Still in defib," Cate said. "Let's deliver another one hundred and fifty joules, then change compressors again. Oxygen clear?"

"Clear," Davian said, removing the mask from the King's face and stepping back.

"Clear." Cate pressed the button on the machine and the King's body jerked again. "Shock given. Resume compressions."

Davian and Noah switched places and the cycle began again as sirens approached from the dock.

Soon, the EMTs boarded and took over, continuing the CPR and getting a rundown from

Cate while hooking up an IV with saline and glucose and giving the King a dose of amiodarone as well. Cate stepped back to allow them to intubate the King then watched as they loaded him onto a gurney and raced him off the yacht to take him to the nearby hospital.

"Cate, I'm sorry I—"

"Don't worry about me. Go!" she said, helping his mother over so Davian could take her hand and lead her off the ship. "I'll check in with you later to see how he's doing."

Even though Davian was a highly trained physician himself, everything changed when it was your loved one on the table. Cate had seen it many times before and she empathized with him. But the King was in the best hands now and they would do what they could to save him.

"Mommy?" Adella asked, coming up beside Cate as she and Noah cleaned up the mess they'd made during the resuscitation. "Will the King be all right?"

"I don't know, sweetie," she said, honestly. They'd caught his cardiac arrest early, but given his medical history, that might not have been enough. For the first time since the emergency had started, her emotions began to surface, and her chest tightened with unshed tears. For Davian and his family and what they were going through now. She blinked hard to keep them at bay, scowling down at the supplies she was gathering up and putting away. Against her wishes and against all odds, Davian had gotten into her heart again. She loved him. But even that might not be enough. "Whatever happens, sweetie, you and I will be there for Davian and the Queen."

Adella hugged her around the neck, the sweetness of it making Cate tear up even more. "I miss Davian."

"I do too, sweetie."

She needed to tell Adella the truth.

Not right then because everything was too crazy. But soon.

First though, they had to get off the yacht and catch their flight home to Boston.

The next several hours were touch and go for the King.

Davian stayed by his father's bedside, holding his mother's hand, and trying to make sense of it all. The day had not gone as he'd planned at all. After the difficult talk with his parents, he'd felt buoyant, like any untethered balloon finally able to fly into the sky. But now, that familiar weight of guilt and responsibility was back.

Worse, he missed Cate and Adella something awful. But he'd had no right to ask them to stay. And his place was here at present, at least until his father's condition had improved or...

Either way, this was where he was needed right now and so he sat there, waiting for news on his father's prognosis. They'd gotten him stabilized at least, and had run numerous tests, with little information as to why his heart had stopped. Some of the cardiologists speculated it had been a stent they'd put in during his bypass. Others thought perhaps a medication issue or chemical imbalance brought on by stress.

Whatever the reason, Davian had been on the phone to the palace and his brother in Ruclecia, alerting them to the situation. Even now, his brother was taking steps to become the interim leader of the country in his father's stead, until the King recovered.

If my father recovers...

It was just the previous year they'd been through all this before, with his heart surgery. Davian had thought that would buy his father at least another decade of good health, but apparently not. His poor mother looked wan and worried and rightfully so. Davian knew from his own medical experience that of cardiac arrest patients whose arrests were witnessed, only 50 percent ever left the hospital again. And with his father's medical history, the odds were significantly worse.

Still, if money could buy anything, it was the best medical care possible, and Davian still had hope. They'd extubated him and the King was breathing on his own now, just still unconscious. His father was strong, despite his age and his medical setbacks. Otherwise healthy and stubborn as a mule. He and Davian went round and round over subjects they both cared about and had different ideas about the monarchy and their place in it, but in the end, they loved each other. He wanted his father to get well, not just for himself, but for his dear mother too. They'd been married over forty years.

Davian couldn't imagine losing a partner after that long. What if that had been Cate lying there...

My Cate...

"Your Highness?" One of the cardiologists gestured from the private hospital room's doorway to Davian. "May I speak with you a moment, please?"

He kissed his mother on the cheek and released her hand, then walked out of the room to the nurse's station with the other physician. "How is he doing?"

"Remarkably well, actually, given his age and his history," the cardiologist said. "His heart is pumping normally again, which is good, and his breathing is regular. We'll need to do more tests once he wakes up, but I'd say your father is a very lucky man."

Relief washed over Davian like rain. "Thank you, Doctor. What's his prognosis then?"

"Well, as I said, there are more tests to run and I'm sure his royal doctors back home will want to watch him like a hawk for the next few months to make sure this doesn't happen again, but as for now, he should be fine to leave in the next few days, once he wakes up. I'll have a better idea of exactly when that will be once he's conscious again."

"Okay. Anything he should avoid until he gets home?"

"Stress, mainly. And that goes for even after he's back in Ruclecia," the cardiologist said. "Your father is nearly seventy now. It's time for him to consider pulling back, delegating some of his royal duties to the next generation."

"Agreed." Davian gave a curt nod. This was the moment his brother had trained for his whole life. "Thank you again, Doctor."

"My pleasure." The cardiologist smiled. "I'm sure we'll speak again before the King is discharged."

Davian returned to the hospital room to tell his mother about what the cardiologist had said.

"I'd told him for years he needs to relax and let Arthur take over." The Queen sniffled and squeezed the King's hand through the bars on the side of the hospital bed. "Perhaps now he'll listen to me."

"Perhaps so."

"Oh!" The Queen gasped. "He squeezed my hand back!"

"Did he? Do it again." Davian watched while his mother held his father's hand tighter and sure enough, his father squeezed her hand back. "That's excellent. Means he's waking up."

The Queen leaned in to kiss the King's fingers and smiled. "Come back to me, my love."

Davian's chest tightened. Speaking of love…

"Excuse me for a moment, Mother." He went back out of the room again and down the hall to a small private waiting area for the ICU guests. There, he pulled out his phone and sent Cate a text, updating her on his father's condition, then asking her a very important question.

Will you and Adella come visit me in Ruclecia?

CHAPTER FOURTEEN

CATE DIDN'T GET the message until they arrived back in Boston, what with all the chaos of connecting flights and keeping Adella occupied and happy. It was early the next morning, and they were in a cab on the way to her mother's house in Medford, northwest of downtown Boston. Adella was asleep in her lap, and when Cate pulled out her phone and unlocked the screen, it took several moments for her tired eyes to adjust to the tiny text and read what it said.

Davian's father had made it and was expected to make a full recovery. That was wonderful. Cate scrolled down farther, stopping at the last line of the message as her own heart skipped a beat.

Will you and Adella come visit me in Ruclecia?

The way they'd left things between them was still very much up in the air.

They still had so much to talk about, so much to decide—about their relationship, about Adella's future. Cate still needed to talk to Adella about who Davian really was. More than anything though, she needed to get out of her own head about it and talk to her mom about it all.

If anyone could give her perspective on things, it would be her mom.

Maya Neves, Cate's mom, was waiting for them when they arrived. She welcomed them home with hugs and a pot of fresh coffee for Cate and hot cocoa for little Adella. They had toast and waffles in the kitchen, then Cate took Adella upstairs for a nap before returning for a private talk with her mother.

She told her about seeing Davian again and them reconnecting, about Cate telling Davian that Adella was his, and the King's cardiac arrest before they left the yacht.

"He invited Adella and me to visit him in Ruclecia," Cate said, staring down into her coffee mug.

"Are you going to go?" Her mother raised a brow at her. At sixty-two, her mother still looked fifteen years younger than that, with a bright, infectious smile and green eyes the same shade as her daughter's. Her mom's hair had gone silver though, giving her a bit of an ethereal look these days. "I mean, he is still a prince, even if it's only by blood. Could be fun to see his palace."

Cate chuckled. "I'm sure it's a very grand palace. I remember seeing pictures of it back in residency when I was trying to get ahold of him about my pregnancy."

The reminder of everything they'd been through put a bit of a damper on Cate's good humor. "I don't know, Mom. It's been a lot happening in a short period of time. And when you're on the yacht, it's like its own little universe. Everything feels heightened there. But now that we're home, what if things have changed?"

"Doesn't sound like it has for him, since he invited you to visit him halfway around the world."

She sighed. "I know. But what if it was just residual adrenaline from the emergency with his father? I'm sure Davian is exhausted from that and dealing with his mother and his family business in the aftermath. He probably needs a good night's sleep and time to think. I know I do."

"Hmm." Her mom sat back, mug cupped in her hands and expression thoughtful. "Well, just don't think too much, Cate. I know you. And you'll think yourself right out of it."

Cate frowned but couldn't deny her mom might be right. She was a first-class overthinker. Always had been. "I just... I'm scared, okay? I got burned once before with him and I survived. Not sure I want to take that chance again. And it's not just me now I must worry about. It's Adella too. I haven't told her anything about Davian yet, so please don't bring it up in front of her until I give you the all clear."

"I won't say anything to her about him yet."

They sat there for a while, the only sound the ticking of the old clock on the wall, until finally her mother asked, "Do you love him?"

"Yes. But I'm not sure that's enough."

"It's a lot." Her mom sat forward again. "Look, honey. I hope this isn't about me and your dad."

She looked up from the table to her mother. "A little, maybe. He walked out on us without a word. He left us to fend for ourselves."

"True, but I wouldn't have had it any other way."

"What?"

"Why would I want a man to be here, in our lives, if he wasn't committed to us? If we weren't the top priority in his life?"

"But you struggled so much, raising me alone. He could've helped with bills and food and—"

"If I'd needed help with that, I could've gotten food stamps. And I did a few times. But financial security is no reason for a marriage." At Cate's dubious look, her mom snorted. "Fine. Not the most important reason. Your father and I loved each other once upon a time, but not the way we needed to for things to work. Sometimes you must let that go to get what you really need and want and deserve in life. You need a man in your life, a father for Adella, who is all in, Cate. Someone who will be there for you through thick and thin. Perhaps your Davian could be that someone for you."

"I don't know, Mom," Cate said, shaking her head. "I'm scared. I don't want to get hurt again."

"I get that, honey. But you'll never find out if you don't give him a chance."

Cate sighed. "You're right. It's just so hard. Letting him close again, after everything that happened between us."

"I don't want to tell you what to do one way or another," her mother said, leaning her hips back against the edge of the counter and crossing her arms. "Lord knows I made enough mistakes in my own life. But please, honey. Don't let your father's actions in the past dictate your choices going forward. The day I broke free of those chains was the best day of my life. I pray it's the same for you, Cate."

"But what about companionship? You've been alone ever since. Don't you get lonely, Mom?"

"Yes, sometimes. But then I have you and Adella and all my friends in the neighborhood. You are only alone if you choose to be. And that's a fine choice to make if it's the right one for you. I did fine on my own, with you. We were two warriors against the world, you and me. And I think we were closer for it. But that doesn't mean the same choice is right for you." Her mother reached across the table and took Cate's hand. "Now, I've never met your prince, and I only know what you've told me about him, but he sounds like a good man. Devoted, dedicated, caring, supportive, loyal. And it seems to me that those qualities extend from his family to you and Adella now too. Your father was none of those things for us, but please don't think he and Davian are anything alike. If you love him as you say you do, I think you need to at least go and see him. If you don't, you'll regret it the rest of your life."

Cate took that it and turned it over in her mind as she had everything else over the last whirlwind two weeks, until finally exhaustion took over and she yawned. "I think I need a nap before I decide."

Her mom smiled. "There's my smart girl. A nap is always a good decision."

"Thanks." She got up and rinsed her cup in the sink then kissed her mom's cheek as she passed her on the way to the door. But when she got up to her room, instead of going to bed right away, Cate pulled out her phone and sent a text back to Davian before she lost her nerve. For better or worse, her mother was right. She needed to go and see Davian once more to see if this thing between them was real or not. And Adella deserved to see her family's homeland.

Tell me when and where and we'll be there. Glad your father's doing better. Cate.

"So, can I call him Daddy?" Adella asked two weeks later when she and Cate were sitting on a plane in Athelas, the capital city of Ruclecia, waiting to disembark. "Or do I have to call him Prince?"

"Well, I think Daddy would be fine, but that's something you two should decide together once we get to the palace," Cate said, undoing her seat belt then reaching over do the same to her daughter's. "But first, we need to get our luggage and find the car they've sent for us."

The captain announced that first-class passengers could exit the plane first, so Cate stood and grabbed their carry-ons from the overhead bin then took Adella's hand to lead her off the plane. She rarely splurged for such luxury travel herself, but Davian had handled all the arrangements for them, so Cate had had little say in the matter. Though she did appreciate the extra legroom and amenities first class offered, especially when Adella was treated to warm cookies and a set of golden wings from the pilot.

They thanked the crew and walked down the gangway to the terminal. Cate hoped she'd be able to find the driver without too much trouble, but it turned out her fears were unnecessary. As soon as they walked out into the gate waiting area, a man in a chauffeur's uniform rushed up to them and quickly guided them through customs, then down the corridor to the baggage claim area. Good thing too, since apparently the paparazzi had been alerted to their arrival as well and were bustling around them, snapping photos and calling out questions. Cate held Adella's hand tighter and quickened her steps.

"Just ignore them, sweetie."

"But Mommy? Why are they following us?" Adella asked, her nose scrunched. "And they keep calling me Princess. You told me I shouldn't call myself that back home."

"That's true," Cate said, pointing to their bags on the carousel so the driver could grab them. "But here in Ruclecia, it's a bit different."

"So, I am a princess here?"

"You're always a princess to me, sweetie." Rather than risk tiring her daughter out so soon, Cate bent and swept the little girl up into her arms and followed the driver out a nearby revolving door to where a black Bentley waited near the curb. The driver stowed their luggage in the trunk and held the door for Cate and Adella to get in the back seat then hurried around to slide behind the wheel. All in all, Cate thought it was probably the fastest trip through an airport she'd ever had. Guess there was something to say for being royal after all. Or at least royal-adjacent.

The drive to the palace took them through the glittering downtown of Athelas then out into the suburbs and finally into the lush green country-side of Ruclecia. There were mountains in the distance and a grayish mist near the ground, re-minding her somewhat the Scottish Highlands or Switzerland. Every so often they'd pass a farm or a quaint cottage.

"Look at the cows, Mommy!" Adella pointed them out, her nose plastered to the window to catch all the scenery rushing by them.

It had taken a while for the idea of visiting Da-vian here to settle in with her, even though Cate had accepted his invitation right away. But in the end, she couldn't bear the thought of never seeing him again, even if he didn't feel the same way about her or want a future together. And the fact was, Adella needed a father. Cate hadn't given up entirely on her plans to start a GP practice ei-ther, but now she had widened her scope. Noth-ing was set in stone, but depending on how this visit went, she might choose to move to Ruclecia instead. Start a practice here, perhaps work in conjunction with Davian's hospital, if he was amenable to that.

They'd texted back and forth a lot the past few weeks as her and Adella's trip neared, discussing plans and arrival times and such. Davian had been busy catching up with his patients and his work as administrator of the hospital. Add to that the fact that his father had recovered enough to finally make the decision to step down and turn the throne over to his son, Crown Prince Arthur. Davian had decided to have their visit coincide with the announcement so that it would hopefully overshadow the news of Adella being Davian's daughter. They'd both decided a more gradual introduction to royal life would be the best for their little girl and hopefully coming now, with so much else going on, would distract from Cate and Adella's presence.

The crowd of press at the airport, however, made her think twice on that subject.

Nervous butterflies took flight inside Cate, but as they rounded a turn in the highway, and the onion-domed cupolas, tea caddy tower and pointed spires of the royal palace came into view in the distance, she knew it was too late to turn around and run. They weren't in Boston anymore, that was for sure.

"Mommy! Look!" Adella gasped. "It's just like my playhouse at Grandma's!"

"Yes, it is," Cate said, smiling. Built on the site of an original castle from the 900s, this version of the royal palace was done in the Romantic historicism style by one of Davian's ancestors in the mid-1800s. And soon, they'd be staying there. Unbelievable. "Are you excited, sweetie?"

"I am!" Adella clapped. "Do you think I can sleep in one of those towers?"

Cate laughed. "Sweetie, I think anything is possible at this point."

CHAPTER FIFTEEN

THAT NIGHT, AS his father came to the end of his speech, Davian stood near the edge of the dais and gazed out at the assembled crowd. It was filled with various politicians and celebrities, as well as the usual glitterati of Ruclecian society. However, he'd yet to spot the two people he wanted to see most in the world. Cate and Adella. He'd been told by staff that they'd arrived safely at the palace earlier that afternoon, and if his schedule hadn't been completely crazy and overpacked with important appointments and patient visits, he would've gone to see them before the reception tonight. As it was though, he'd barely made it here on time himself, only finishing with his last responsibilities about fifteen minutes before his father took the stage.

"And so, it is with great nostalgia and hope for the future of our great nation that I humbly resign as your monarch and turn the throne over to my eldest son, Crown Prince Arthur. Thank you."

His father took a short bow toward the crowd that had erupted into applause and shouts of "God save the King." King Phillipe was looking much better these days. And while the cane he used to walk with now would probably be a lifelong companion after the nerve damage suffered to his leg following the cardiac arrest on the yacht, his color was good, as were his lab results. In fact, if he kept going on with his healthy habits, he might well outlive them all.

The King made his way offstage as Crown Prince Arthur took over the mic to give his acceptance speech, and Davian was there to help his father down the short set of stairs. Their relationship, while certainly better than how they'd left things on the *Querencia*, still held a bit of tension and chill to it. Davian hoped one day they could resolve their issues with one another and, if not accept their differences wholeheartedly, then at least get back to the friendly relationship they'd had prior to the cruise. But honestly, if this was how it had to be for Davian to have his freedom, he could live with it.

"Thank you, dear," his mother said, kissing Davian's cheek. "You are so wonderful, always looking out for us."

His father grumbled and straightened, pulling free of Davian's helpful grip. Still stubborn, as always. "I am not an invalid, son. I can walk by myself."

"Of course, Father," Davian said.

"And where are these guests of yours?" his father asked, giving his youngest son an arch stare, trying to goad Davian into another argument. "The doctor and her daughter."

But tonight, he wasn't taking the bait. "I think you mean Cate, the woman I love, and *our* daughter, Adella. And the answer is, I'm not sure. I was told they arrived safely, but I haven't had time to see them yet." Davian searched the crowd around them again, without success. "In fact, if you don't require me, I think I'll go and find them."

"Run along, dear," his mother said. "Go find your lady love and bring her back here. I've so much to talk to her about."

"And I want to get a look at this granddaughter of mine," his father added, surprisingly Davian.

"Be back," Davian said, kissing his mother once more on the cheek before weaving into the spectators to try to find Cate. He found them near the back wall, Adella playing with the stuffed octopus he'd bought for her at the aquarium. He couldn't fight the wide grin blossoming on his face and didn't try. Damn, it was good to see them again. For the first time in weeks, he felt like he could breathe again.

"There you are!" He walked over and without waiting, pulled Cate into a hug. She felt wonderful in his arms, warm and strong and real. "How was your trip in?"

"Great," Cate said, pulling back to run a hand down the skirt of the ball gown she wore. Everyone was dressed formally for the occasion—Davian in a tux, like the rest of the male guests, while his father and brother were dressed in their finest military regalia. The shimmery seafoam green color of Cate's gown set off her eyes and blond hair to perfection, also highlighting her tanned skin. She went to say more but was interrupted by a tug on her hand.

"Mommy?" Adella asked, in a whisper loud enough for Davian to hear with no problems. "Can I say it now?"

Cate took a deep breath, glancing from Adella to Davian then back again. She nodded and Adella squared her little shoulders, then dropped into a cute little curtsy. "Hello, Daddy."

Davian feared his heart would trip right out of his chest and land in a puddle of goo at his daughter's feet. It was the first time Adella had called him that and he wanted to remember the moment forever. He bowed to her, then crouched, putting them at eye level. "Hello, Princess. I'm very glad you're here."

"Me too." She smiled at him, clutching her octopus tight. "Can I call you Daddy? Or should I say Prince? I asked Mommy, but she said I had to talk to you about it first."

"Well…" Davian swallowed hard against the sudden lump of emotion in his throat. "I think Daddy has a really nice ring to it."

"Yay!" With that, Adella launched herself into his arms and hugged him tight around the neck, her stuffed toy squashed between them as he stood with his daughter in his arms. "I've always wanted a daddy and now I have one and you're a prince too and I'm so excited to show you all my toys and maybe we can play together and then you can read me a story at bedtime. Do you like stories, Daddy? I love them and…"

He caught Cate's eye over the top of Adella's head and saw her fighting hard not to laugh at his astonishment. He'd dreamed of this moment going well, but never imagined Adella taking to him so quickly or so enthusiastically.

Cate stepped closer to whisper, "She's been eagerly awaiting seeing you since I told her the truth a few weeks ago. She always liked you, even on the yacht, so when she found out you're her daddy, it was icing on the cake. Good luck!"

"Thanks." He chuckled.

"So," his father's voice said from behind him, causing Davian's pulse to stumble. Their little family might be new, but Davian already vowed to fight anyone, friend or foe, who tried to take it from him. Including his father. He turned slowly, Adella still chattering on obliviously in his arms, to find his father, scowling over at them from a few feet away. "We meet at last."

"Phillipe," his mother said, coming up to take his father's arm. "Perhaps we should wait…"

"I've waited long enough," the old King said, stepping closer with his cane to squint at Adella, who was now staring back at him too, wide-eyed and curious. The King's bushy gray eyebrows knitted. "What do you have to say for yourself, young lady?"

Adella squeaked and Cate stepped closer, apparently feeling as protective as Davian at that moment. Then their daughter cocked her head and squinted right back at the former King of Ruclecia. "My name's Adella Neves and I'm a princess. And you look like King Lars!"

Davian's father blinked at the little girl a moment then glanced at Cate. "I am unfamiliar with this ruler."

Cate bit her lips again. "He's on her favorite TV show, *Elena of Avelor*. It's a cartoon."

"Oh." The King seemed puzzled by that for a moment, then looked at Adella again. "He must be very handsome and kind and wise then."

"He is," Adella said, seriously. "But it's more about your fancy medals."

Davian and his mother and Cate all stared at each other a moment then burst into laughter simultaneously while his father straightened, and Adella held on to her octopus tighter. Then, finally, his father cracked a smile and, even more surprisingly, began to laugh as well. Big, full belly laughs that Davian hadn't heard from the man in years, decades even. It was refreshing and went a good way toward mending bridges between them.

Then his mother moved forward to smile at Adella. "You look just like your father at that age. You're five, aren't you?"

Adella, now shy, nodded, chewing on a stuffed tentacle.

"Well, I'm your grandmother, Arabella," his mother said. "May I hold you?"

Adella's expression turned wary. "I already have a grandma. Her name is Maya."

"You can have more than one, sweetie," Cate said, stepping in beside Davian to rub Adella's back. "We talked about this. Queen Arabella is your grandmother too. And King Phillipe is your grandfather."

"Really?" Adella looked between the two older people suspiciously.

"Really," Davian's parents said in unison.

"Oh." Then, just as suddenly as she'd taken to Davian, his daughter wanted down to go over to his parents. "In that case, can you show me the stage up front, please?"

His mother looked at Cate, who nodded. "Just don't let her talk you into eating all the sweets at the refreshment table. She's already had enough for one night."

They watched his parents walk away, Adella holding their hands between them.

"So," Davian said, after a moment. "Would you take a walk with me?"

She nodded and they went out a side entrance to the main ballroom to a small private balcony overlooking the royal gardens below. When Davian had been a boy, this was one of his favorite spots to sit and think by himself. Few people came out here, and he wanted to share it with Cate now. Especially since he had something very important to ask her.

"It's lovely out here," she said, leaning over the granite railing. The air had turned colder this November but was still refreshing after the stuffy ballroom.

Davian couldn't get enough of seeing her tonight. The slight blush in her cheeks, visible in the light from the sconces on the wall. The softness of her green eyes. The sweet floral scent of her perfume. Cate looked up and caught him staring and Davian looked away fast, heat prickling his neck from beneath the collar of his starched white tuxedo shirt.

"How was your trip in?" he asked, flustered by her nearness in a way he'd never been before.

She laughed softly, the sound wafting around him on the slight breeze. "You asked me that already, Davian. What's got you so on edge?"

"I…" His hand brushed against the small box-shaped lump in his pocket and his pulse tripped. This wasn't like him. He was always cool, collected, calm under pressure. But whenever he was around Cate, all that went right out the window. *Just do it. Just ask her.* He took her hand and brought it to his lips to brush a kiss across the back of it. "I need to ask you a question."

Cate turned to face him, her expression quizzical. "Okay."

Davian took a deep breath for courage and reached into his pocket for the little velvet box he'd stashed there earlier, creaking it open to reveal the sparkling emerald cut diamond engagement ring inside.

"What are you…" Cate frowned, her free hand trembling as she covered her lips with her fingers. "Davian."

Now that he'd started, he couldn't stop. Not until he heard her answer. "I love you, Cate. I always have. From the first time we met back in residency until tonight, you've knocked me off my feet in the best way. I lost you once, and nearly lost you again after the yacht charter. I don't ever want to lose you again. Will you do me the supreme honor of becoming my wife, Cate Neves?"

With that, he got down on one knee and held the ring up to her.

Cate's breath caught and her lovely green eyes filled with tears as she smiled. "I love you too, Davian. Even when you were David. I'll always love you."

Then Davian was standing and slipping his ring onto her finger, and they were kissing, soft and sweet, a promise of more—much more—to come. When he pulled back, resting his forehead against hers, they were both grinning. "That's a yes, right?"

She giggled and nodded then kissed him again. "Of course, it's a yes."

Three months later...

Cate and Adella were back in Ruclecia, permanently this time, and Davian couldn't have been happier. They were all at the grand cathedral in Athelas for his brother's official coronation as King of Ruclecia. His parents were there too, as was Cate's mother and his brother's wife and children, the soon-to-be Queen and Crown Prince and Princess of Ruclecia. Outside of the royal family, the pews were filled with friends and well-wishers, international guests and celebrities and all the major news outlets.

His brother had struck a bargain with the tabloids. The palace would provide regular updates and selected photos for their use in exchange for privacy outside of that. For now, the agreement seemed to be holding and for that, Davian was glad.

Even more encouraging was the fact that the palace security team had managed to capture and arrest all the members of the radical group behind the assassination threats made against the royal family. They would still be cautious because they'd all lived that way so long it was hard to break the habit, but a huge weight had been lifted off Davian and his brother. All of them were expected to be convicted based on the overwhelming evidence that had been compiled against them.

All was well in Ruclecia again.

"Mommy?" Adella whispered, squirming in her seat between her mother and father. "Will I have a fancy dress like that in June?"

Cate tracked where her daughter was pointing to Arianna, Arthur's daughter and Adella's royal cousin. She smiled. "If you want, sweetie. You're going to be the prettiest flower girl regardless."

"Cool!"

Davian bent to kiss his daughter's head, then Cate. They were planning their wedding, and while Davian no longer participated in official royal duties around the country, the people still loved him and all he did to help keep the people of Ruclecia healthy, and they demanded a large spectacle of a ceremony.

"And what kind of dress is your mommy going to have?" he asked, slipping his arm around Cate's shoulders and pulling both her and Adella closer.

"Whatever kind of dress fits by then," Cate said, laughing as she placed a hand over her small baby bump. They were expecting another child, though they were keeping it a secret for now. "Your mother, the Queen, said she still had her old wedding dress, so we might try to work that in somehow. She'd like that, I think."

"I'm sure she would," Davian said, leaning in to kiss his soon-to-be wife's cheek again.

Adella slipped out from between them and leaned over to glance down the pew to where her grandparents were all sitting together. She'd adjusted well to their recent move and life in Ruclecia and was currently being spoiled rotten by all her grandparents. "Can I go sit with them, Mommy?"

Cate sighed, then nodded. "Fine. But hurry. And be quiet so you don't disturb the ceremony."

Adella hurried off, leaving Davian and Cate alone. He snuggled her closer, more content than he could ever remember being. They were working together at the hospital and building a new life together at home. What more could a man ask for? "Happy, darling?"

Cate tucked her head into the crook of his neck and gave a happy sigh. "Beyond happy, my love."

* * * * *

If you enjoyed this story, check out these other great reads from Traci Douglass

A Mistletoe Kiss in Manhattan
Their Barcelona Baby Bombshell
Island Reunion with the Single Dad
Costa Rican Fling with the Doc

All available now!